Still Yours

Written by

Cara Roman

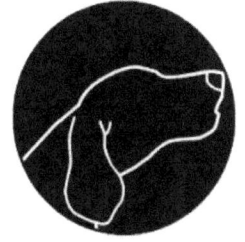

Baying Hound's Dark Side
USA

Disclaimers and Copyright

Still Yours

Copyright © 2018 by Cara Roman

All rights are reserved.

Published by Baying Hound's Dark Side

ISBN: 978-1-955670-00-5

To my own fleeting first love all those years ago, these scars you left in your wake as you burned brilliantly through my life taught me more than I could ever explain. For that I will always be grateful. And to the voices that sang on repeat in my earbuds while I wrote this love story, thank you for flooding my soul with so much inspiration. You will never know how much you have given me.

Prologue

It was a muggy night, the stickiness lingering even after the sun went down, and off in the distance there were fireflies dancing in the dark. Sitting on the front porch steps Leigha didn't notice their blinking lights though. She kept staring at the old beat-up truck idling rather loudly in her driveway. Feeling like her heart was disappearing inside of her chest. Even as naive as she still was at eighteen years old, she had always known deep down that Ridge wasn't really meant for this tiny Midwest town. His dreams were far bigger than everything else around here, and even she felt them constantly pulling on him. She was starting college next month and had figured she at least had that long. They were on borrowed time though, and she could admit to herself that she would always be wishing for another day with him no matter when he left.

Leigha had tried her very best not to fall in love with him two summers ago when Ridge started coming around all the time to flirt with her. But she had tumbled over the cliff into that swirling abyss despite all the warning bells going off in her head. As she fought the tears burning behind her eyes, she remembered that very first kiss. Sitting on the tailgate of that very same truck staring into his clear bottle green eyes because they were infinitely more beautiful than all the colorful fireworks shooting up into the July sky up above. Ridge had softly tucked an errant strand of her deep brown hair behind her ear and leaned his head slowly down towards hers giving her plenty of time to turn away. Instead, she had closed her eyes and tipped her head up to meet his. His lips had felt warm and soft against hers, and Leigha had opened her mouth eager for more. As soon as his tongue had touched hers the rest of the world just melted away, and in that moment, she was irrevocably his, forevermore.

Now that the end she knew was always coming was finally here Leigha was completely powerless to stop it. Staring up into the eyes that she knew better than her own she couldn't let him see her heartbreak. All Ridge had ever wanted was to move down south to Nashville and chase his dreams of being a country singer. He had worked the last few years delivering pizzas, baling hay, milking cows, even cleaning out stables. Basically, doing whatever he could to set aside enough money to leave. It wasn't some spur of the moment decision; his whole life had been marching up to this.

The bed of his truck, the one that she had given up her innocence in on a folded-up flannel blanket last summer, was stacked with everything he owned in this world except his guitar. That was in the front seat, sitting in what she had always considered her spot. Even love couldn't compete with a dream like that. Whenever Ridge's hands weren't on Leigha, they were on the strings of that guitar. Leigha couldn't even muster up any jealousy for that instrument, because it was half of the reason, she finally agreed to go out with Ridge in the first place. Sitting in a plastic lawn chair across a blazing bonfire she stared at him, as he sang song after song. She could still see his face lost in the music he was making, and she was mesmerized. Her heart fell at his feet in that moment, and there was nothing she could do to stop it.

The moonlight was bathing Ridge's profile as he sat next to her, his hands tucked into his front pockets. The faded red t-shirt with their high school logo stretched tight across his broad shoulders. His golden-brown hair, shades lighter than hers, was flopping mischievously down into his eyes like usual. Leigha leaned over, laying her head on his shoulder and took a deep breath, pulling his fresh scent with the hint of spice deep into her lungs. Ridge pulled a hand out of his pocket and laced his calloused fingers with hers.

"Once I get settled you can transfer to a school down there. It shouldn't take long, you'll see. Only be a few months, then we'll be together again Sugar," Ridge said. His deep voice rumbled softly.

She could hear the hope clear in his voice. He was trying to convince the both of them. "You're going to make it, Ridge. I know you will."

Ridge stood up, pulling Leigha up off the porch steps with him. She wrapped her arms around his neck, his hair tickling her fingertips. He stared down into her eyes for what felt like hours, but Leigha knew was only just moments. Ridge leaned down, kissing her, his arms holding her body tight up against his. Pulling back, he sent her a lopsided smile, the one he knew was her favorite, tugged the ends of her hair playfully, and walked across her front yard to his truck. He climbed into the driver's seat, slamming the temperamental door behind him. He stuck an arm out the window in a wave and pulled out of her life as the tears she couldn't hold back anymore finally streamed down her face.

Leigha sat out on the porch steps for a long time after Ridge left, feeling as if the moment she actually stood up and walked inside it was all going to be real. He was really going to be gone. When she finally walked brokenly into the house both of her parents were sitting in the dim living room. There were tears pooled in her Mom's eyes, and when her Dad looked up at her she saw the helplessness echoed in his eyes. He couldn't fix this pain for her, no matter how much he wanted to. Leigha kept moving past them, needing to be alone. Heading up the stairs to her bedroom. Laying down on her bed she curled into a ball and emptied her soul out one tear drop at a time.

Chapter One

The overhead bell dinged as she walked in the front door. Leigha really loved that tinkling sound greeting her every morning. She pulled chairs down from atop tables as she walked towards the counter in the back. Snagging her apron from the hook she always kept it on Leigha wrapped it around her waist twice tying it neatly in front. Pulling her long hair back in a low ponytail with the elastic always on her wrist, she booted up the computer to the cash register. Grabbing a bag of coffee beans off the shelf stacked with them she turned on the grinder. The smell of freshly ground coffee beans filled the place, and Leigha smiled, inhaling the scent deep into her lungs. That deliciously intoxicating smell had never gotten old for her, and every single day of the last five years it never failed to bring a smile to her face. She was nearly done setting up for the morning when Dani rushed in, late as always. Her blonde hair high up in a ponytail bouncing as she rushed past Leigha, her arms loaded with bakery boxes.

They had been best friends as far back as

either could remember. There wasn't a memory from her childhood that didn't have Dani in it. "Sorry, Silas couldn't find his other shoe this morning, even though it was exactly where I told him it was." Dani shrugged her shoulders and reached for her apron.

"That boy would lose his head if it wasn't attached," Leigha said with all the love in the world. Silas was Dani's eight-year-old son, which made him her honorary nephew. Dani scooted past her and made her way back into the kitchen. Leigha heard the radio switch on, and automatically winced as the achingly familiar voice floated out front towards her. Dani was quick to turn the volume down, but Leigha had already heard it. The pride she felt at hearing Ridge's songs playing on the radio constantly warred with the gaping hole he had left inside of her. A few minutes later the volume turned back up when a new song came on. Shaking her head at Dani's kind, but wasted effort Leigha yelled back, "Whatcha got today? I'm about to make the specials sign."

"Blueberry streusel cookies, along with all of the usual assortment," Dani shouted back out.

Leigha wrote the special flavor of the day on the countertop chalkboard she had made herself. Five years ago, this was just a terrifying dream of theirs. This little spot squeezed between a salon, and a pharmacy downtown was in rough shape. The diner that used to be in the space had been closed for years. The two of them had scrubbed, peeled, painted and patched it all up themselves. They had both worked their fingers to the bone that first year desperate to keep their heads afloat. Things were easier now, and they had even managed to hire some part time help.

Leigha was just turning over the open sign at 8am, when Dani carried out a tray with her beautiful cookies ready to be loaded into the display case in the front counter. The first customer of the day was Mrs. Bowman. She had been coming in three days a week like clockwork, since the very first day they opened. Somewhere north of seventy, nobody dared ask, she used to teach second grade at the elementary school in town. She was everyone's favorite teacher, whether you actually had her or not, and while she sat in front of the front window eating her cookie and drinking her coffee, people inevitably came in off the sidewalk to say hello and chat with her. Leigha had always wondered if Mrs. Bowman did that on purpose, drumming up business for them, or if it was just a lucky happenstance.

Just before lunch time Tina came in to help run the front counter. As usual Tina got the cash register and Leigha filled orders. At only twenty years old Tina was full of energy and exuberance. Leigha could still remember babysitting her not too long ago, but that was the way it went in small towns. Everyone was connected to each other through a string of memories. Her life was consumed by her boyfriend, and social media. It always made Leigha feel old and brittle somehow, but she could admit that wasn't really Tina's fault.

Filling coffee orders was second nature to Leigha by now, working all those years through college as a barista. Thinking back, at the time it was just a job so she could afford the gas to get to and from classes. She spent more time waiting on calls from Ridge than on her studies freshman year. She was still so full of hope for his dream, and love for him. But as the time went on, he called her less and less. He always seemed so busy that even when they talked it was all about his life, what gigs he was booking, or who he was jamming with down in Nashville. By her sophomore year his name had stopped appearing on her phone, and Leigha realized that Ridge was finally lost to her. He'd gotten swept away by his dream, just like she had always feared he would be.

With nothing else to do Leigha buckled down

and concentrated on her classes, finding time to study was easy to do since she had no social life to speak of, and couldn't sleep most nights either. Ridge's big break came during the fall semester her junior year, and suddenly he was absolutely, unavoidably, everywhere. They hailed him as country music's next big thing. The radio stations played his song every single hour, catapulting him into stardom like he had always dreamed of. Their small town was understandably very proud of him, and it was all anyone could talk about. At first Leigha all but burst she was so full of happiness for him. But he felt so far out of her reach now, and that first glowing rush she felt at his success couldn't patch up all the holes that kept appearing in her heart.

When Leigha graduated with her degree in business and got a job at the bank in town she figured this was her life now. It only took two years for Leigha to completely and utterly loathe working at the bank. Even the sweater sets and blazers she had to wear made her skin crawl. But the big wakeup call had been sitting behind her boring desk one morning seeing the big front page newspaper story announcing Ridge's engagement to the pretty blonde country sweetheart Suzy Cordell. Not that settling down at twenty-four years old was shocking, I mean

Dani had been married for a few years herself at that point. But deep down Leigha still always thought of Ridge as hers. That tiny, but bright spark of hope had been lighting the darkest corners of her despair until it sputtered out as she touched his smiling face in the picture. They were the 'it couple,' blazing up the country music charts together, and the whole industry, and world, was in love with their picture-perfect fairy-tale romance.

That night as Leigha drove home from the bank stuck on autopilot she saw the empty diner and figured, what the hell. Feeling like there was only one way from here, and she decided that it was going to be up. Leigha turned towards Dani's little house instead of her own. Sitting on her friends couch she told her she was going to open a coffee shop. She had been so much happier back when she was fixing other people's coffee than she ever was at the bank. After she was finished with her big plans Dani quietly confessed that her husband Jason was cheating on her, and he told her he was leaving to be with the woman he met online. They cried together over a bottle of wine, and knew it was time to take control of their lives. This was not who they were meant to be! And Caffeinated Sprinkles was born somewhere in the wee hours of the night.

The very next day Leigha filed the paperwork for a loan, and they never looked back. Working all day at the bank, then pulling an all-nighter getting their space ready gave Leigha something to focus on as the frenzy of Ridge and Suzy's wedding reached its fevered pitch. Dani baked cakes in the grocery store she worked at during the day, picked Silas up from daycare and baked cookies all night trying out recipe after recipe.

It took them almost a year to get the doors opened, that was five years ago though. At thirty Leigha finally felt like she wasn't living in the cold and empty shadow cast by Ridge Bradley anymore. She figured it was about damn time too, since it had been twelve years since his truck had roared out of her life.

Chapter Two

Leigha was back in the kitchen helping Dani box up a couple dozen special order cookies scheduled for delivery after they closed for the day, which was in about a half an hour. Tina was out front probably bored with nothing much to do, it was basically dead when she walked back to help Dani. The overhead bell dinged, and Tina let out a rather loud giggle, and a breathlessly shaky, "Oh my god, hi! Umm, what can I get for you?"

Confused, Leigha glanced over at Dani immediately who said, "Oh, he wouldn't dare."

"Who?" Leigha asked, even more confused, but Dani was already storming out of the kitchen into the front. Leigha followed along, though not with Dani's anger fueled burst of speed.

"You sure have got a lot of nerve Ridge Bradley! Thinking you can come in here, after not setting foot in this town for over a decade! I heard you were coming back, and hoped it was just a nasty rumor, I'm real sorry to see I was wrong," Dani said heatedly.

Leigha stopped in her tracks with her hand

up, ready to push the kitchen door open and felt the world grind to a shuddering stop beneath her feet. Ridge was here, in her shop, on the other side of that door, after all this time. Standing there frozen in place, barely daring to breathe, she listened to his response.

"Hey Dani. Guess I deserved that, God knows I probably deserve even more," Ridge said. His voice was deeper than it used to be, finally settling into the husky rumble it had only hinted at back when he was eighteen years old.

"You've got no idea how much more," Dani stubbornly tossed back.

"I didn't mean to start anything by coming in here, honest, I was just wandering around town, and before I knew what I was doing I was walking through the door. It's really nice to see you though Dani, and this place looks really good."

"You seem to have a habit of not knowing what you're doing until it's too late. Tina's already got your coffee, and it's on the house, if you get the hell out before she wonders what's going on and comes out front," Dani said.

Leigha turned away from the door, pressing her back to the wall, desperately needing to feel something solid.

"Fair enough, you two always did look out for each other. Can you tell her that I said, well that I was, just tell her that I'm..." Ridge couldn't settle on what he wanted to say. Leigha could almost see his expressions as he struggled to find the words. But the face she pictured was stuck twelve years in the past, and not what she knew him to actually look like now. But there was not enough curiosity in the whole world to make her peek through that window at him and take the chance he would spot her.

"Uh-uh. Nope. I'm definitely not going to tell her anything for you. And you really shouldn't either! Don't you think that you said plenty a long time ago? Go on back to your picture-perfect life with your picture-perfect wife and leave her the hell alone. You've done it so very well all this time," Dani shot back.

"My divorce was final a few months ago," Ridge said quietly. "This is a small town Dani, we're going to end up running into each other." Leigha barely heard what Ridge was saying, her mind kept repeating the first part on an endless loop as she tried to process the information. Divorced? Divorced! Divorced.

"What are you playing at Ridge?" Dani asked.

"Absolutely nothing. It really is nice to see you

again Dani," Ridge said just before the bell dinged and he walked out the door.

Leigha was still leaning up against the wall when Dani walked back into the kitchen. Dani took one look at Leigha and walked over pulling her in for a hug. Leigha rested her head on Dani's shoulder like she had so many times in her life before. "You knew he was back in town?" she whispered.

"Yeah, well I heard he was coming back. Didn't know he was already here. Thought I would have time to let you know beforehand," Dani said pulling away shaking her head.

"I'm not the girl he left behind, I'm a grown ass woman who owns a business now," Leigha told her friend.

"I found you leaning up against the wall and shaking like a leaf," Dani reminded her gently.

"True. But it's not like I expected him to walk in here. It was kind of a gut punch. Now that I know, it won't happen again," Leigha said with determination.

"How much of that did you hear?" Dani asked with a worried look on her face.

"Everything," Leigha said. "How did he look Dani?" She couldn't stop herself from asking. The words poured out without Leigha even meaning for them to.

"Honestly? When hasn't Ridge looked great? But there is a hard edge to him now that I'd not seen on him before," Dani said. "But I've seen it in the mirror a time or two myself. Divorce will do that to you."

"Oh, honey." Now Leigha pulled Dani in for a hug. "Giving you up was the stupidest thing Jason ever did."

"Thanks, Leigha. I know I'm better off, honestly, I do. But it's really hard not to be disappointed sometimes that I picked someone who let me down so bad," Dani said wisely.

"I highly doubt Ridge feels disappointed that he picked Suzy," Leigha said, and even to her own ears it had the sickening ring of bitterness to it.

"Nothing is ever exactly what it seems." Dani shrugged. "Do you want to get out of here and drop off those cookies?"

"No, you go on ahead, it's on your way to pick up Silas from the sitters anyway," Leigha said. "You've got the kitchen cleaned, all I really have to do is count down the till, since Tina usually cleans out front. Go, I'll be fine, really I will. Although you did make a rather fine knight in shining armor, my dear," Leigha said with a wink.

"Anytime you need me I'll saddle up my trusty steed," Dani joked as she picked up the boxes.

They walked out front together and Leigha helped Dani load all the boxes into her car. Leigha waved at her best friend as she pulled away from the curb and walked back inside. She turned the lock behind her, and flipped the open sign hanging from the door over to closed. Tina rattled on about how exciting it was to have Ridge back in town as she swept and mopped the floors. Leigha tried her best to tune the girl out. She understood that Tina was only eight when Ridge left, so to her he was just someone famous who used to live there. The whole town was probably in a right tizzy about it. And why shouldn't they be? It wasn't *their* heart he had forgotten about all those years ago. To everyone else Leigha was just the girl Ridge used to date back in high school.

As Tina left for the day, her phone was already up to her ear excitedly talking to her friends about seeing *the* Ridge Bradley at work. Leigha took out the till and shut down the cash register for the night. Carrying the till back to the office she sat down at her desk to count it out. Leaving only enough money in it to be able to make change the next morning she carefully tucked the rest into the zippered bank pouch. Locking up she grabbed the small box of cookies she had set aside earlier and walked out to her SUV.

Leigha drove the block and a half across town to the bank. Going through the only stoplight in town, and it wasn't even the kind with three different colors, it was only a blinking four-way. She made it a habit to make small deposits every day after work, that way there was never any money sitting around the shop. After she deposited the days earnings, and made the expected small talk to everyone she headed out of town to the house she had grown up in. As soon as she walked up the familiar front steps her Mom opened the door and hugged her.

"Oh, baby, how are you? I was grocery shopping earlier and Ridge being back home was all anyone could talk about," her Mom asked pulling away to look in her brown eyes, and reading everything written in their depths. "You saw him already." Moms always knew everything.

Leigha walked in and set the box of cookies down on the kitchen counter. She told her Mom all about Ridge stopping in her shop earlier. "I couldn't even make my feet carry me through the damn kitchen door Mom. I ended up hiding from him like a loser." Leigha yanked the elastic out of her long hair in frustration.

"Well, I'm sure it was quite the shock. There is no shame in needing a few minutes to absorb it all and catch your breath," her mom said trying to ease the pain.

"At least I didn't lose it in front of him," Leigha said running her hands through her hair.

"Would that really be so bad though? If he had to face how much he hurt you?" her Mom asked quietly.

"It doesn't matter anymore Mom. And I definitely don't want him to think I've been holding on to him, pining away all these years while he moved on and had this full happy life without me," Leigha said, her voice catching. "I haven't been waiting around for him to come back, I haven't. I gave that up about a decade ago."

"Of course you did honey. Just remind me again, how long has it been since you went out on a date with a man?" her mom asked tilting her head to the side.

"Not as long as you think. And it's because nobody has interested me enough to bother. Not because I'm crying into my pillow over my stupid high school sweetheart." Leigha sighed. It had been at least six months since she'd gone out with a man, and that date hadn't been much to write home about. Watching her date check his phone all night for the football score and not bothering to pay attention to their conversation, so much so that Leigha had spouted off nonsense just to see if he would notice. He didn't. But the final nail in that coffin was when he walked her to her car after dinner and tried, rather forcefully, to kiss her anyway.

"I'm not sure anyone ever gets over their first love, and yours burned brighter than most," her Mom said patting her hand sympathetically.

"You never had to get over yours," Leigha said with a smile.

"And thank God for that," her Mom laughed. "Are you staying for dinner honey? I'm making meatloaf tonight."

"Nah, I've got to get home, but give Dad my love please, and make sure he shares some of those cookies with you," Leigha said with a wink knowing her father's sweet tooth, and stood up pressing a kiss to her Mom's cheek before leaving. Talking to her Mom hadn't fixed anything, but it still made Leigha feel better.

Chapter Three

Ridge had been in town for a full week now and Leigha really tried to be grateful to have avoided running into him around town so far. But with each passing day it felt more like a ticking time bomb waiting to detonate, and it had her on edge. She knew it wasn't a matter of if she would see him in a town this small, but when. The constant wondering if this was the time as she walked into the gas station, or the grocery store, left her thinking it would be infinitely better to get it over with quickly, like ripping off a band-aid. He was the most exciting thing that had ever happened here, and now that he was back his name was on the tip of every tongue. Everyone who came into Caffeinated Sprinkles asked her if she had seen him yet. The first few times she shook her head no, but that seemed to make people uncomfortable. Feeling like she was going to end up being the talk of the town—*'poor Leigha still waiting on Ridge'*—she started answering that he had been in and loved the shop. After all, it was technically true. Ridge had been in, and he had told Dani that he liked what they had done with the place. Leigha just conveniently omitted that she wasn't a part of that particular conversation. The answer seemed to satisfy everyone who asked, and then thankfully, the conversation could turn to other things.

Mrs. Bowman was holding court, as usual, in front of the window, telling anyone who would listen that Ridge had stopped by her house for a visit. Leigha caught herself smiling as the old lady happily chatted about what a good boy Ridge had always been, completely glossing over all the mischief he had gotten up to as a young boy running around town. The gossip turned to speculation on why Ridge was even back in town in the first place. There was never a father in the picture, and his mother had moved away to live with her sister shortly after Ridge left to chase down his dreams. Nobody blamed Diana Bradley for leaving, there was nothing left tying her here anymore. With nothing holding him to this town, someone said they thought Ridge was back home to nurse his wounded heart after the public divorce. Which had made Mrs. Bowman tip her head back and laugh before shaking her head at the silly notion.

But the thought stuck in Leigha's head, Ridge's heart being so shattered that nothing could heal like the home he left so long ago struck a nerve deep within Leigha's chest. Knowing how bad her own heart ached not too long ago that wasn't something she would wish on anyone. Lost in her own thoughts, the rest of the day flew by. Tina wasn't scheduled today, which left Leigha to handle the cleaning up at closing time. Dani's domain was the kitchen, and she always left it completely immaculate when she left. Leigha closed out the cash register and shut all the machines off. She put all the chairs up on the tables and cleaned the floors. Untying her apron, she hung it from the hook and headed back to the office while the floors dried to count out the day's earnings.

Her phone buzzed, looking down she saw a text from her neighbor inviting her over for dinner. That was the last thing she needed. Ty had been trying to make a move on her for quite a while now, and she just couldn't think of him that way. He was a dependable man, hardworking, funny, and devastatingly hot. In another lifetime it would be a complete no-brainer. But all she could see when she thought about it was Ty standing next to Ridge laughing in his varsity jacket by the bank of lockers in high school. Or sitting next to Ridge in the bleachers, his arm slung around her, both of them cheering as they watched Ty win his wrestling match. They were all friends in back then, and in her mind, no matter how much she tried to, she couldn't extricate the memory of Ridge from their dynamic. Picking her phone up she replied back "*maybe some other time.*" If her Mom knew she was brushing off another eligible man she would never hear the end of it, but Leigha would worry about that later.

Grabbing her purse and tucking the zippered bank pouch holding the daily deposit safely inside Leigha walked out of the office. Even dropping the money off at the bank, it took her less than fifteen minutes until she was pulling into the driveway of her house. It was a cute little single story brick ranch tucked on a side street in town, that had been painted a quiet cream with cool brown trim. There was a little garage, and a big front window overlooking the postage stamp sized front yard. Unlocking her door, she walked from the garage to the cozy kitchen and set her purse down on the countertop. Pulling her hair out of the elastic she gave her head a shake, letting it fall wherever it wanted. Her cat Finn weaved in and out of her legs demanding attention. Bending down she picked up the slim orange tabby. Nuzzling his face a moment before she scratched behind his ears just the way he liked.

"How was your day Mr. Finn?" Leigha murmured. Finn rumbled his response, purring happily in her arms.

Walking from the kitchen into the living room Leigha settled down on the couch with Finn in her lap. Sitting there long enough that Finn drifted off into a contented nap Leigha contemplated what to make for dinner. She understood why Ty invited her over, cooking for one was moderately depressing most of the time. If that was all it was she would have gladly accepted just for the company. But Leigha couldn't pretend she missed the look in his eyes. He was being patient so far, but he was definitely looking for an opening. Tucking one leg up under the other she wondered why she couldn't just be happy with that. The answer was plainly clear though, she wanted a love like Ridge made her feel when she was eighteen. Settling for someone just because he would fit nice into her life would never be enough. How could it? She knew what it meant to be consumed by the feelings burning inside of her. To look into someone's eyes and forget how to breathe. And no matter how broken he left her heart in the end, when Ridge had held her close, she knew he felt it back then too.

Running her hand through her hair Leigha sighed and wished, not for the first time in her life, that she could turn it all off and not feel things so deeply. Finn stretched and crawled off her lap to walk to the other end of the couch and give himself a bath. Leigha walked back into the kitchen and pulled the door to her refrigerator open surveying the contents inside. Pulling items out she stacked them on the counter. A green pepper, some mushrooms, an onion, the carton of eggs, and a bag of shredded cheddar cheese. She was just opening the cupboard for a frying pan when there was a knock at the front door. Walking back out to the living room thinking it was probably Ty coming over to see if he had better luck with his invitation in person, she didn't even glance out the window before swinging the door open. And all the breath left her lungs in a whoosh as she saw Ridge standing on her little front step. His hands were tucked into the pockets of a pair of faded blue jeans, he had on scuffed boots, and a plain black t-shirt. She blinked silently at him for a couple of seconds before her mind would actually form thoughts.

"Hey Leigha," he said softly. There were lines etched into the corners of his eyes, and his jaw looked sharper than when he left. But his brown hair looked like he had forgotten to get it trimmed, just like it always had.

"Ridge," Leigha said. "What are you doing here?"

"In town?" he asked with a tilt of his head.

"No, at my door," she replied. Seeing him there in front of her after all these years instead of hurting like she thought it would, just felt kind of strange. Like it was happening to someone else and she was watching it play out.

"Would you believe me if I said I was in the neighborhood?" Ridge said with a lopsided smile. Leigha shook her head. He went on. "Nah, didn't think so. I guess I just wanted to see you."

"Well, here I am. Pretty hard to lose me, I've been here all along," Leigha said. Ridge winced, he covered it up quickly, but she had seen it before he smoothed his features out again. Something about that unguarded expression surprised her, and before she could think better of it, she stepped back. "Are you hungry? I was just about to make myself an omelet."

"That would be good, thanks," he said stepping inside, the surprise clear on his face. She saw him glance around taking in her space before she turned away and headed to the kitchen. Finn jumped off the couch eager to make friends. "Hi there fella," Ridge said squatting down to pet her cat.

"That's Finn," she called out.

In the kitchen Leigha took a deep breath, grabbed a knife out of the block and started chopping the vegetables. Ridge walked in and leaned against her counter watching. Doing her best to ignore his eyes on her, she turned the burner on under the pan. Leigha cracked eggs into a bowl, and whisked them briskly, adding in just a touch of milk. Judging the pan to be hot enough she slid a bit of butter in, and picked the pan up sloshing the melting butter all over the surface. Satisfied she poured in the eggs. Turning she caught Ridge's eyes as she grabbed the silicone spatula out of the ceramic pot on the counter. Steeling her nerves, she turned back to the stove and watched as the eggs cooked. Judging them ready she sprinkled in the chopped veggies, added some cheese before folding the top of the omelet over. Picking up the pan with one hand she grabbed a plate down from her cupboard with the other. Sliding the omelet onto the plate she handed it to Ridge without looking.

"Silverware is in that drawer there," she gestured, before turning back to make hers. She heard the slide of the drawer opening and closing.

Then she heard the scrape of the chair at her little table as Ridge sat down. "Do you want a beer?"

"If you're having one, sure," he said.

Leigha repeated the same actions making her omelet. Once it sat steaming on her plate, she set the pan into the sink. Grabbing two bottles of beer out of the refrigerator she walked over to the table. Setting her plate down across from Ridge she noticed he hadn't touched his food yet waiting for her and had set silverware out for her too. Fighting a smile at the manners his mother had all but pounded into his brain, she held one of the bottles out to him. His hand brushed hers softly as he took it, sending little chills up her arm. Ignoring it, Leigha stepped back quickly and sat down. She watched as he twisted the top off and took a pull from his drink and found herself unable to tear her eyes away from the muscles working in his throat as he swallowed.

"How did you know where I lived?" Leigha asked a few minutes later.

"Mrs. Bowman. I didn't ask, if that's what you're thinking. She basically filled me in on all the happenings in town she thought important. Your address was on the list," he shrugged and brought his fork up to his mouth taking a bite of food.

"Of course she did," Leigha said thinking she

probably should have figured that out when she heard Mrs. Bowman had Ridge over for a visit.

"Jason left Dani?" Ridge asked sounding surprised. He was surely remembering back to school when Jason followed Dani around like a lovesick puppy dog.

"Yeah, a few years ago. Ran off with some woman he met online leaving her to raise Silas all on her own," Leigha explained eating her own dinner.

"Shit. Does he send her support at least?" Ridge asked, knowing what it was like to grow up fatherless with a single mother.

"About a year after he left, she got a check for a hundred dollars. But when she tried to deposit it in the bank, they told her he didn't have sufficient funds to cover it," Leigha said feeling angry all over again. "CS is doing well now though thankfully, so they're not hurting financially."

Ridge nodded his head understanding what she wasn't saying. They were making it without Jason's help, but that didn't mean there weren't struggles. "Seems like you've got a real good thing going with that coffee shop."

"Thanks, we're pretty proud of it," Leigha said.

Their food was finished and Leigha stood up

from the table to take care of the plates. Ridge stood up too, and picked his up before Leigha got the chance to grab it. Leigha didn't argue, if he wanted to carry his own plate to the sink, let him. She turned the water on and ran her plate back and forth underneath the spray rinsing it off. She felt Ridge standing behind her as he reached around and set his plate under the water. He wasn't quite touching her, but he was close enough that the heat from his body was making hers feel empty as it ached to reach out for his warmth. She watched as he turned the water off, and with his hands lightly on her hips he turned her around to face him. Looking up into his green eyes Leigha could see his plans written in them. As his head leaned slowly down to hers, she tried to step out of his arms, but her traitorous feet refused to move. His lips touched hers softly, tentatively at first, unsure of their welcome. Leigha opened her lips on a gasp and he took full advantage. His tongue swept into her mouth, tasting exactly the same way it had all those years ago. Unable to fight it Leigha slid her arms up his neck and into his hair. Gripping the strands in her fingers, she held on for dear life and kissed him back.

Ridge growled down low in his throat, and the sound filtered through the haze covering Leigha's brain. Pulling her mouth away from his she shook her head, anger sizzling around her.

"What? Did you think that you were so great way back when that I'd want you again now just like that? Oh look, Leigha's still single, so she'll fall right back into my arms. And how long would that last before you got bored and wandered off to find another superstar to warm your bed forgetting about me completely?" Leigha said dragging a shaking hand through her hair, wrapping herself up tightly in anger to avoid all the feelings his kiss had stirred awake within her.

"That's not it at all. Shit, I know I shouldn't have done that Leigha," Ridge said stepping further away from her. Leigha felt the distance with every ounce of her being. Ridge tucked his hands back in his pockets, this time she knew it was to keep them off her, and said "I wish you knew how many nights I've lain awake with your name playing in my head like a song stuck on repeat." He swallowed a few times, looking like he was going to say more, but then he shook his head and walked out of her house.

Leaning against the counter Leigha held a shaking hand up to her mouth realizing that she wanted to call him back with everything inside of her.

Chapter Four

Leigha didn't get any sleep, moving around her bed restlessly all night. The shadows dancing on the wall teasing her imagination. There was no denying the chemistry bubbling between the two of them. Leigha could accept the fact that Ridge was always going to call to her on an elemental level. Just that one kiss left her body aching, and no matter how many times she tried she couldn't ease the need raging inside of her. When it came down to it a vibrator just wasn't the same thing. Sure, it hit all the right spots, and usually worked in a pinch. But running your hands over warm, sweat slicked skin as a man moved deliciously deep inside your body, wasn't something anyone had managed to replicate yet. Somewhere around five in the morning it occurred to her that she was the one stopping it. If she had let him Ridge would no doubt be laying next to her now. She just had to figure out a way to keep her heart out of it. That was all. They could burn this sexual tension out of their systems, and finally be past it. After all, there was no way he could be as good in reality as he was in her memories, or the fantasies currently swirling through her brain.

Giving up on sleep Leigha got out of bed and walked to the bathroom. Turning on the shower she brushed her teeth while the water heated up. Grabbing a towel, she sat it on the counter and pulled the shower curtain back stepping into the hot spray, letting the water beat down on her head silencing her thoughts. Focusing only on the task at hand she washed and conditioned her hair. Running a razor over her skin she carefully shaved. By the time she turned the water off and stepped onto the thick absorbent rug in front of the tub she felt better. Now that the decision was made all the nerves fell away. All that was left now was following through, and that would be the fun part.

Wrapping the towel around herself, tucking an end up to hold it she reached a hand up and wiped the fog off the mirror. Staring at her reflection she wondered what Ridge would think of the changes in her body. The years had been kind to her, but even still, thirty looked different than eighteen had. Running a wide tooth comb through her long hair, so dark from the water it was nearly black. She carried about ten more pounds than she did back in high school, most of it in the breasts that had grown a full cup size, but her hips were also wider than they used to be. Thinking about the way she had changed had her wondering about Ridge, what had time done for him? Just thinking about it was sending a delicious shiver of anticipation through her body. Determined to not go there again she picked up the tube of moisturizer and squeezed a dollop in her hand before smoothing it onto her face in gentle upward strokes.

Back in her bedroom she turned on the light, earning her a rather vicious glare from where Finn was curled up on the bed. Laughing at him, she opened drawers pulling clothes out. The jeans were some of her favorites, well worn, and would be comfortable all day at work. Pulling up the sleeves of her turquoise Henley to just below her elbows she sat down on the bed to slide socks onto her feet. Walking back into the bathroom she pulled the hair dryer out from the cabinet under the sink. Turning her head upside down she switched the heat on. Running her fingers through her thick tresses she flipped her head to the left and to the right. When her hair was about three quarters of the way dry, she wrapped the cord back around the blow dryer and put it away. Picking up her deodorant off the counter she reached inside her shirt and applied it. Checking her reflection in the mirror she nodded her head and walked out of the bathroom. Leigha rarely bothered to wear makeup. Hiding the freckles that kissed the skin of her nose and cheeks made her feel like she was wearing a mask to hide who she was. Her lashes were already dark, and she tended to forget about it when she put mascara on and rubbed her eyes making a mess of it anyhow. Tucking a tube of her favorite minty lip balm in her pocket she walked out of the bathroom.

In the kitchen she poured food into Finn's bowl, and refilled the water in the bottle that made sure his bowl was always full. Grabbing her purse off the counter she walked back into her room to get the phone she accidentally left in there, spotting the stack of library books she needed to return. Picking those up Leigha called out a goodbye to sleepy Finn as she headed out the garage door to her car. Even stopping by the library to drop the books off in the afterhours return slot she was a full half hour early getting to her shop. Unlocking the door, she walked inside and turned the machines on needing a cup of coffee herself after the sleepless night she had. By the time Dani walked in Leigha had already had two coffees and was practically buzzing on caffeine.

"Well don't you look ready to tackle the day," Dani said as she headed back into the kitchen her arms stacked high with bakery boxes.

"Ridge came over to my house last night, I didn't get any sleep, made him dinner, had two coffees already, he kissed me, with extra shots of espresso in them, I'm going to sleep with him to get it out of my system and get over him I think, since my trusty vibrator wasn't enough," Leigha blurted out barely taking a breath as she followed her friend into the kitchen.

"Whoa, hold up. And slow it down a little. Ridge came over last night?" Dani asked turning around to face Leigha, her eyes practically bugging out of her head.

"Yep. Just showed right up at my door. I thought it was Ty knocking on my door at first to invite me to dinner since he texted me earlier, but nope. He wants to be with me, ya know," Leigha said bouncing on the balls of her feet.

"Who? Ridge or Ty?" Dani asked laughing at Leigha now.

"Ty. I don't know why Ridge kissed me. Got me all worked up though, and I spent all night trying to work him out of my system. But my vibrator just isn't the same," Leigha explained like it was obvious.

"Jesus Leigha, from one kiss?" Dani asked clearly impressed.

"Nobody kisses like Ridge does. He literally melts my insides to goo," Leigha said breathlessly.

"Okay, I can see that. He has always been off the charts hot. But won't having sex with him complicate things? Bring up feelings you fought so hard to lock up?" Dani asked gathering ingredients and setting them on the stainless-steel table in the middle of the room.

"I'm not worried about that. We're just strangers now, who used to be in love when we were kids," Leigha said shrugging. "He told me that my name plays in his head at night when he can't sleep."

"Oh yeah, this isn't going to get complicated at all," Dani muttered as Leigha scooped her hair back into a ponytail and walked back out front. "Salted caramel mocha nutella brownies today!" she yelled out front to Leigha's back.

"Ooooo, I'm so going to need at least three of those pronto," Leigha shouted back as she scribbled it on the chalkboard sign.

"Maybe start with one first? They pack a punch," Dani said carrying them out to the display case. "I'm in the mood to make white chocolate raspberry cookies too, so I'll let you know when those are ready."

"Do you know where Ridge is staying?"

Leigha asked.

"Nope," Dani said gliding past her back to the kitchen. "Why?" she asked poking her head back through the door.

"So I can go over and seduce him of course. C'mon, try and keep up Dani," Leigha laughed bouncing on her feet.

"Not sure I want to." Dani shook her head as she poured ingredients into her giant mixer.

Chapter Five

The caffeine buzz that kept her flying high all day was just starting to fade as Leigha walked out of the bank at the end of the day. Her determination to flush Ridge out of her system was still hanging around though, and she had paid extra close attention all day to the gossip. Leigha headed out of town towards where she heard Ridge was most likely staying, although nobody had actually been out to visit him yet. The houses out here were tucked into the forest, far enough apart that you couldn't see your neighbor's house from your own. As she pulled into the long drive her hands started trembling slightly while she gripped the steering wheel. The house was sitting at least a quarter mile back, and you couldn't see it from the road at all. The property bridged the best of both worlds, comforts of your hometown, with complete privacy and seclusion. She could see the appeal of that for Ridge, with him shining bright in the spotlight so often it probably felt good to power down and recharge.

Ridge was lounging on a swing on the wide front porch, the same old acoustic guitar in his hands, looking a little more beat up than when Leigha had seen it last. He had a flannel shirt on with the sleeves rolled up, and a pair of jeans with a ripped knee she could tell he hadn't bought that way. One leg was up, his booted foot resting on the porch railing. His head was tipped down towards his instrument still, but his guarded eyes met hers the moment she stepped out of her car. That was new, he had never looked at her with the shutters drawn before, and she wasn't sure that she liked it. The car door shutting echoed loudly, the sound bouncing around the tall trees surrounding the yard like sentries. A large chocolate lab was laying at Ridge's feet, he watched her happily, his tail thumping in obvious welcome.

"Whatcha doing out here Leigha?" Ridge asked, his green eyes burning into hers even across the distance.

"I wanted to talk to you about last night," Leigha said stopping at the bottom step and wrapping an arm around a column to hold herself back from charging up to him. "Your dog is beautiful."

"If you're thinking on chewing me out again no need. I got the message clear enough yesterday. I won't be apologizing for kissing you though. I shouldn't have, I've no right to put my hands on you anymore, but I'm not going to lie and say I'm sorry I did it, because I'm not." Ridge looked down at the dog who was whining excitedly. "Go ahead and say hi to her Boomer."

The lab jumped up and raced down the steps to Leigha, planting his butt in the grass probably to stop himself from jumping on her excitedly, tail swishing with joyful abandon as she rubbed his head. Petting Boomer for a few minutes helped Leigha gathered her courage. All he could do was say no, and she would leave, no worse off. Right? Right. "That's not it Ridge. I didn't get any sleep last night because I wish I hadn't stopped you."

Ridge sat up straighter in the swing, removing his leg from the railing, he watched her, his arms resting loosely over the body of the guitar, but there was an awareness in his body that wasn't there a moment ago. "I'm gonna need you to be more clear, darlin'," He said.

Taking a deep breath Leigha took a step closer. "I can't stand here and act like there isn't chemistry bubbling between us. Still. We both know that kiss wasn't lukewarm."

"Nope, sure wasn't. We always had plenty of heat." Ridge nodded his head in agreement.

He didn't add more, so Leigha carried on. "I don't have anyone in my life right now, and I don't see why I should deprive myself of something that I want," Leigha said climbing up another step.

"What is it you want?" Ridge asked setting the guitar down on the swing next to him.

"You, Ridge. I want you. I want to feel your hands on my body," Leigha said softly. "No commitment, no promises, and no heartbreak this time," she said looking up at him, and holding her breath.

"You're asking me for just sex?" Ridge said standing up slowly.

"Until neither one of us wants it anymore," Leigha said nodding her head, and finally stepping up onto the porch.

Ridge ran his hand through his hair, and shook his head. "And if that's not enough for me?"

"That's all that's left between the two of us," Leigha said stopping barely a breath away, so close she could feel the heat from his body beating against her senses. Staring up in his eyes she saw the moment he made his choice, which only a heartbeat before his arms wrapped around her, crushing her against his chest and his mouth unerringly found hers. Leigha reached up around his neck, her fingers finding their way up into his thick brown hair. Ridge's tongue slid hungrily against hers, and she reveled in the taste of him. His hands gripped her ass, pulling her even tighter against his body, letting her feel his desire, and Leigha needed to feel all of that body against hers. Now.

"Too many clothes," she whispered as she peppered to kisses across his beautifully masculine square jaw.

"C'mon," Ridge said grabbing her hand and leading the way inside. There were boxes stacked in towers all around, and he was clearly in the midst of unpacking still. He dragged her past a living room towards the large staircase leading up to the second floor. Halfway up the stairs he turned to kiss her again, like he just couldn't take another second without his lips on hers. Caught up in the rush of passion, Leigha moaned into his mouth.

Holding her face in his hands he pulled away. Running his thumb across her lips he stared down at her. The look in his eyes made Leigha worried he would stop them now, so she said, "Take me to your bedroom Ridge." He nodded his head slowly before turning and walking the rest of the way up the stairs. Leigha barely got more than an impression of the house as she walked down the hall, because her eyes never left Ridge's strong back. His shoulders had gotten broader, and the muscles moving in them as he walked held her in a trance. He turned, walking through a doorway, as soon as Leigha followed him into the room he shut the door. She looked questioningly up at him.

"Boomer," he said. Leigha remembered the dog then, and nodded her head understanding. Nothing ruined the mood quite like an interruption from a pet.

Ridge reached behind Leigha and pulled the elastic out of her hair. Free of the band it fell in heavy dark waves down to the middle of her back. Tangling his fingers in her hair Ridge tipped her face back so he could plunder her mouth. By the time he pulled away Leigha's skin was on fire, her nerve endings singed by the blistering heat building between them. Impatient to feel his skin she reached out and unbuttoned his shirt, when she got to the last button she slid her hands along his skin and pushed the flannel shirt off him, grateful he wasn't wearing another shirt underneath. It fell to the floor and she stared at the wide expanse of his chest in front of her. There was more dark hair peppered across it than the last time she had seen it. Running her hands over him she learned him all over again.

Urged on by her hands on him Ridge pulled her top off and sent it flying across the room. Pushing her back against the door he kissed from her shoulder to her collar bone, tugging the strap of her black bra down as he went. Needing more, she reached back and unsnapped the bra to give his wandering mouth more access. With a knowing smirk he pulled the bra away from her body. She felt the heat of his gaze as it raked across her breasts, making her shiver eagerly in anticipation.

Instead of feasting on the banquet in front of him like she expected he reached down and undid her jeans, pushing them slowly down her hips. Dropping down to kneel in front of her Ridge pressed a soft kiss against the front of her black panties. His hands slid slowly up, and he finally cupped her breasts. His eyes were locked on her own, watching them melt at his touch. Looking down at him Leigha gasped as his tongue licked slowly over the lace barely covering her. His calloused thumbs circled around her nipples and she moaned, leaning back against the door for support. Her hands gripped his hair as he meticulously worked the panties against her clit. The friction of the lace added a delicious new edge to the sensation. Leigha was panting already, her heartbeat racing. He reached out and tugged her panties down with one hand, the other still playing with one of her nipples. Free of the barrier between them, she felt his tongue glide across her already quivering clit for the first time in over a decade. He sucked the sensitive bud into his mouth, and her hips bucked helplessly against his face. She felt the scrape of his teeth, before he licked it gently again. Her body started shaking as he quickened the pace, his tongue remembering the exact pattern she needed. Tossing her head back on a cry Leigha came in a hot rush. Ridge licked her slowly, savoring each of the little aftershocks as they pulsed against his mouth.

Standing up off his knees Ridge reached down and picked Leigha up, knowing her wobbly legs wouldn't be able to support her weight after that orgasm. He carried her across the room. Setting her atop the large bed he reached down and unbuckled his belt. Licking her lips Leigha watched him slide the leather slowly through the loops. When it was free, he let it fall to the wooden floor with a loud thump. He unbuttoned his pants and dragged the zipper down in a way that let her know his bulge was straining against it. Hooking his hands in the jeans and boxers she watched him push them down and step out of them. He stood there in all his glory, wearing nothing but his skin. Seeing his long, thick dick for the first time in so many years had her mouthwatering. Leigha remembered exactly how good that had always felt inside of her, so good that nobody else had ever even come close. Sitting up she reached a hand out to stroke down his length. The rumbling moan escaping his lips encouraged her to lean her head down for a taste. Holding the base, she swirled her tongue around the tip. Closing her lips around him, she sucked hard, pulling off his dick slowly before sliding back down. She worked him for a few minutes, until she felt his muscles tense, and couldn't take it anymore either. Sitting up she wrapped her arms around his neck and leaned backwards, pulling him onto the bed with the momentum of her body.

Ridge reached his arms out stopping him from crushing her as they fell back into the middle of the bed. His body pressed hers into the softness, Leigha looked up into his eyes, and opened her legs wider in a clear unspoken invitation. Refusing to rush through this, Ridge tipped her head back and kissed her breathless, his dick pressed hotly against her pussy teasing them both. Lifting his head up he looked down at her and moved his hips, finally sliding in exactly where she wanted him. Leigha gasped at the familiar intoxicating feeling of him inside of her. Ridge grinned down at her, and she found herself smiling back up at him before he started moving. The rest of the world disappeared now that he was inside of her, and Leigha gripped his back letting his body do what it always had, and carry her blissfully away from reality.

It didn't take long before the pressure was building inside of her pussy, making her whimper with each and every stroke. He reached down and pulled her leg up higher, his fingers digging deliciously into her thigh. The new angle had him going in even further and Leigha closed her eyes absorbing all the sensations assaulting her senses. With a groan he started moving his hips even faster, but shortening the strokes, working that spot where everything swirling inside of her was centered. Leigha came hard with a scream, her eyes flying open. She looked up, watching Ridge's face as her body broke apart around his. She saw him clench his jaw, groaning, fighting hard to hold it together. Needing him to be just as lost in the moment too, she reached her hands up yanking him down to her, devouring his mouth. Ridge started pounding into her, dragging her pleasure out as he raced towards his. Loving every second she pressed her legs into his sides bringing him in even closer, and she felt his devastatingly accurate rhythm start to stutter. She knew he couldn't fight it any longer. Biting down on his lip as he growled into her mouth, she felt him stop moving deep inside of her pussy twitching as he came in a rush. Leigha smiled, feeling completely and totally satisfied for the first time in years.

Chapter Six

Ridge rolled off Leigha, flopping heavily next to her, both of them still struggling to drag much needed air into their lungs. She leaned up to rest across his warm chest. His arm came around her immediately without any hesitation. His fingers tangled into her hair, playing with it, making the ends tickle along the skin of her back. His eyes were closed, as she smiled down at him saying, "That was perfect Ridge, exactly what I needed."

He opened his eyes, the lush green of them even deeper with the orgasm still singing through his veins. "My pleasure," he said with a flirty quirk of his eyebrow. "So, ah, it occurs to me now that I can actually think straight that we forgot a condom. Is that gonna be a problem?"

"Naw, I'm still on the pill," Leigha said unfazed, tracing fascinating patterns in the hair across his chest.

"That's good," he said on a sigh. "Still?" he asked.

"Yeah, remember I was on it before to help my periods stay regular? Well, I've never gone off it," she said with a shrug. "Not that I make a habit of using it as my only protection. But, well, I figure I can probably trust you with that."

"You can. Too many guys get into music just to bang chicks, but I never really got into bringing random groupies back after my shows," Ridge chuckled.

Nodding her head Leigha changed the subject not really wanting to hear any more. "Sure are a lot of boxes down stairs. How long are you staying for?"

"I bought the house," Ridge said.

"Why? Your whole life is in another state," Leigha asked him confused. She had been sure he was just renting the place for a little while. Get a taste of back home, to regroup, and move along.

"Maybe I realized that you can leave home, but it really never leaves you," Ridge said moving his hand up underneath her hair to caress the skin on her back.

Leigha arched into his touch on a sigh. His fingers skimming along the small of her back felt so damn good. Ridge probably meant what he was saying now, but he would leave again, she just knew it. It wouldn't be hard to sell the house when he changed his mind. Leigha was more convinced than ever to keep this just sex between them as Ridge used a hand on the back of her head to pull her down to his waiting mouth. He kissed her slowly, with lazy satisfaction. But she wasn't finished with him yet and let him taste the hunger that was already blossoming inside of her again. His other arm came around, fingers sliding lightly down the skin on her side. Needing to feel more of him Leigha lifted a leg over his hips and climbed up straddling his waist. Leigha kissed across his jaw, and Ridge turned his head to the side, giving her the access she sought. Licking the sensitive skin of his neck, she felt the air stirring her hair on his shaky intake of breath. Knowing she had him now she scraped her teeth across the skin and up to his ear, before sinking into the lobe and nibbling. His hands grabbed her hips, fingertips digging in, as he groaned. Leaning back Leigha looked down at him as she went fully up on her knees. She could feel how hard his dick already was, just from kissing on his neck, and she rocked her wetness against him enjoying the way it made his eyes go hazy and unfocused.

"Shit, you feel so fucking good," Ridge said his hands roaming everywhere he could reach.

"Yeah I do," Leigha said huskily as she raised her body up, centering him where she needed. Lowering herself down, his thick length slid inside of her achingly slowly, one inch at a time. Moving back and forth slowly she rubbed the swollen head deep inside her pussy. Leigha let out a gasp at how good that felt. The sensations carried her away, and she rocked her hips with complete abandon. Ridge cupped her breasts, squeezing and molding them drawing a long throaty moan from her lips.

"Damn baby," Ridge said, his voice a deep growl.

Leigha looked into his eyes as she rode him, chasing the beautiful bright light flowing through her. Every single breath was ending in a whimper, and she felt like a wire strung too tight. Ridge reached down to where their bodies met, and pressed his thumb against her clit. She started trembling and shaking. Gripping his wrist tightly she came hard with a long, drawn-out cry, stilling on top of him, unable to even move with the intensity of her pleasure. Ridge lifted his hips pumping into her fast and hard. Leigha arched back, her hair tickling the tops of his thighs. Helpless to do anything but absorb each powerful thrust of his dick up into her pussy as her orgasm pulsed endlessly on. Ridge gave a shout and sat up, wrapping his arms tight around her shaking body, his lips finding hers as she felt him come too.

He kissed her tenderly as the thundering heartbeat echoing in her ears slowed down. When he finally laid back down with a sigh she climbed carefully off him. "Bathroom?" she asked. He motioned lazily to a door behind her with his hand. Getting carefully off the bed Leigha paused to make sure she could still remember how to walk before she crossed the floor. After cleaning up their mingled fluids, of which there was plenty after coming so hard, more than once, she walked back out. Looking around she gathered up all her clothing setting it in a pile on the bed so she could put it on easier. Ridge sat up leaning on his elbows to watch her with a lopsided grin on his face.

"I was just gonna order a pizza tonight. Do you still like mushrooms and peppers?" he asked.

"Yeah, but I've actually got to get home." She smiled, unable to resist leaning down to kiss his lips one more time.

"Alright," he said, sitting all the way up to perch on the edge of the bed now. "We gonna do this again?"

"Oh, absolutely," Leigha said tossing a laugh over her shoulder as she opened the bedroom door. Boomer was laying out in the hallway looking bummed to have been banished from the room.

Leaning down she scratched behind his ears. "See you later Boomer." He thumped his tail happily. Standing back up she all but danced down the steps and out the front door. Walking across the yard, just starting to darken with the dusk she climbed into her car. Leigha drove the whole way home with a giant smile on her face, while her skin felt gloriously warm and soft like she had been basking in the sun in the middle of the summer. Ridge was even better than any fantasy, absolutely no comparison. She determinedly paid no attention to the heart she was keeping locked up tight.

Chapter Seven

The spectacular sex with Ridge had Leigha still glowing from the inside out at work the next day. There was a permanent smile affixed to her face, and she was practically dancing as she greeted customers and filled orders all day. Dani didn't even bother asking, it was obvious that Leigha had found Ridge, and burned up the sheets making up for lost time. Leigha knew that Dani was worried she was racing towards a brick wall of inevitable heartbreak, but she just couldn't worry about that right now. If that was what was coming for her then she was going to enjoy this moment. She had survived Ridge once, and this time she would be doing it on her terms, without a broken heart. After all you can't get it broken if you have it locked up tight, right?

Just after the midday rush ended her Mom breezed in with all her usual style. "Hi, baby. After that appointment I deserve some caloric bliss. What magic has Dani got for me today?" she asked leaning over the counter to kiss Leigha's cheek.

"Chocolate chip maraschino cherry

shortbread bars, and orange creamsicle cookies. What appointment Mom?" Leigha asked already getting the tea she knew her Mom preferred.

"Oh, I just had my eyes checked. But you know as well as I do that Dr. Hunt smells like mothballs and talks as slow as molasses in the middle of winter. Tries my patience every single time. And I think I'll go with one of those cherry bars. I'm just going to poke my head back and say hi to Dani while you make my tea, okay honey?" her Mom asked, sliding past her into the kitchen.

"Okay then," Leigha muttered to herself. By the time her Mom came back out of the kitchen Leigha was already setting the tea and snack on the nearest table. "Did you get all the details from Dani, or shall I tell you myself?" she asked knowing exactly what was discussed between the two of them back there.

"Well, Dani only knows what you have shared with her, and it was juicy enough. As your mother I'm not sure I want to know anymore particulars." Her Mom laughed shamelessly, not embarrassed in the least. "What I want to know is whether you've given any thought to how you want this whole thing to play out? Sleeping with Ridge might be a good time, and I'm sure it's a *real* good time, but how long will it stay that way?" her Mom asked biting into the shortbread. She rolled her eyes and made an appreciative *mmmm* sound in the back of her throat as she chewed.

"I know I can't fall in love with him again. He is a leaver, and this town will never be able to hold him for long. But no man has ever made me feel the way he does, physically speaking. I want to feel all of it for once, not just the watered-down version I've made do with all these years. There is still so much heat between us, and I'm going to enjoy this for now. The rest I'll just worry about later," Leigha said shrugging her shoulders sitting down across from her Mom.

"Is it what he wants too?" her Mom asked, cutting straight to what Leigha hadn't said.

"I was very clear on what I wanted from him," Leigha said pulling her hair out of its ponytail to rearrange and put it back up. "He didn't complain."

"Well, no, what man would?" Her Mom laughed, the brown eyes exactly like her daughter's twinkling warmly. "Have your fun, enjoy the hell out of him, but please be careful."

"I will, don't worry about it, Mom."

"That's my job, no matter how old you get, you know that," her Mom said reaching out to squeeze her hand a moment.

"If you say so Mom," Leigha laughed as the sound of the bell jingled as the door opened. She stood up, a smile on her face ready for the customer.

Ty walked up to the counter as she made her way around to the other side. "Hey Leigha. You're looking really pretty today," he said.

"Thanks, this apron really drives all the menfolk crazy," she said with an exaggerated curtsy, laughing it off.

Ty smiled and shook his head slowly. "I'm going to my parent's house for dinner tonight, I'm in charge of dessert, I guess. Got anything I can bring?"

Leigha tilted her head studying him. His eyes were a golden-brown color that reminded her of whiskey in a glass, and his hair was almost as dark as her own. But it didn't fall in his eyes the way Ridge's did. And that was really all there was to it. Shaking herself out of her thoughts she remembered what he had asked. "What about a cookie platter? That way everyone gets to pick exactly what they want. We have chocolate chip maraschino cherry shortbread bars, orange creamsicle cookies, black and white striped, white chocolate macadamia, peanut butter, strawberry jam sandwiches, and mocha fudge drizzles today."

"They all sound pretty good. Dani makes a mean cookie," Ty said shrugging and looking a little bit overwhelmed with his choices.

"That she does. I'll put some of each in there for you. Did you want a coffee while I get it all boxed up for you?" Leigha asked.

"Yeah, that would be great," Ty said leaning against the counter. "I was wondering if you wanted to catch a movie this weekend?"

Leigha grabbed one of their happy mint colored bakery boxes with Caffeinated Sprinkles printed in a pretty navy scroll across the top, while Tina made his coffee. Leaning down into the display case she grabbed cookies arranging them just so in the box.

"I don't think that's a good idea Ty," she said pausing to look up at him.

"You might have some fun, ya know," he said.

"I'm sure I would, but it's just not like that between us Ty. If you could tell me you wanted to hang out as friends that would be a whole different thing, and I would say yes to a movie. Can you say that?" she asked him.

Ty shook his head back and forth, his eyes smiling. "Always so straight forward, Leigha."

Leigha finished boxing up his treats and

handed him the box. Tina had already rung his order up, and he had paid while they were talking.

"We might surprise you Leigha, if you gave it a shot," Ty said with a wistful smile before he turned to walk out.

Leigha just sighed.

"How long have you been turning down Ty Walker? And when were you going to tell me?" her Mom asked from where she still sat at the table.

"A few weeks now. He has invited me over for dinner a few times." Leigha shrugged, impressed her Mom had actually managed to stay silent during the whole exchange.

"Exactly what is wrong with him? He's always been a good boy," her Mom said. "And he is quite handsome now too."

"Yeah, he is a hottie for an older guy," Tina added.

"Mom," Leigha said, while cringing a little at Tina calling Ty old. Her Mom just stared at her waiting for a better response. "It's hard not to think of Ridge when I see Ty. We all hung out in school together. If I could somehow separate him from that I might have given him a chance. But I see Ty and think of Ridge. It's really just that simple."

"And you think you can keep this thing with

Ridge casual after telling me that?" her Mom asked, finishing up the last of her tea with a put-upon sigh. "Well, it's your business, for now. Box up a few goodies for your Dad, he will pout all night if he finds out I came in here and didn't bring him home anything," she chuckled. Leigha grabbed a small box and set a few cookies in that she knew her Dad would like the most. Handing it over to her Mom she leaned in and kissed her cheek. "Just at least make sure you're being honest with yourself, baby," her Mom said patting her hand before walking out of the shop.

Leigha was just closing up for the day as Tina cleaned up when the phone on the wall buzzed. Thinking it might be someone needing to make an order she picked it up. "Caffeinated Sprinkles."

"Hey Leigha." Just the sound of the deep voice on the other end was enough to send chills racing down her skin.

"Ridge," Leigha said leaning against the wall.

"I don't have your number, but this place is listed. I was thinking I could pick you up tonight, have some dinner, and end the night back in your bed." His voice sounded like honey, warm and thick as it slid deliciously over her senses.

"Or, I could come by your place," Leigha said,

remembering last night in his bed.

"And dinner?" Ridge asked.

"I'll just eat before I head over. I got to stop and feed Finn first anyway. See you around eight?" Leigha asked, avoiding it all together.

"It's only four now." She could hear him sigh.

"I know," Leigha said holding the phone against her ear with her shoulder.

"Alright, see you at eight then," Ridge finally said.

"Can't wait," Leigha said with a smile. She heard Ridge's frustrated groan before setting the phone back in its cradle up on the wall.

Chapter Eight

At home Leigha made herself a chicken Caesar salad, and spent an hour playing on her phone while she ate it. Then she made herself sit on the couch and cuddle with Finn. She was the one who told Ridge what time she was coming over, and it annoyed her that now all she wanted to do was jump in the car and speed over there. That wasn't going to happen though. This is ridiculous, she could handle holding out until eight, which was only in an hour. Damn it, standing up she walked into her bedroom impatiently. Today she wore a pair of scuffed up jeans and a Caffeinated Sprinkles t shirt, and as proud as she was of her business it just didn't say booty-call with your famous ex-boyfriend. Pulling the elastic out of her hair she shook it out as she stood in front of her closet. As she scanned the contents her eyes fell on the perfect top. Yanking the current one up over her head she grabbed the hanger off the rack. The slouchy black sweater fell enticingly off one of her shoulders. She had never worn it, but Dani had talked her into buying it insisting that it looked killer on her. Debating only a minute she reached back and unsnapped her bra before tossing it into the basket with her other dirty clothes waiting to be washed. Shrugging into the shirt she walked into the bathroom to look in the mirror. Turning this way and that as she looked at her reflection. The sweater was incredibly thin, and didn't do much for warmth, but that wasn't the point. The jeans were tight enough that they offset the slouchy top, and even without a bra it looked great.

Going bra-less wasn't her normal behavior, but when you're anticipating being naked moments after you get to your destination it worked quite well. Leigha brushed her teeth before leaving the bathroom. Picking up her cell phone she checked the time, nodding she walked over to where he was laying in a chair, and smoothed her hand over Finn's back. "Don't wait up for me Finn, I'm hoping to be late." She smiled picking up her car keys as she walked out the door into the garage.

The night was cloudless, and millions of stars shimmered and winked up in the sky. It was the kind of night made for driving. The air was cool, but Leigha was warm enough in her car without a coat. And after the long winter she was beyond sick of wearing the damn thing anyway. Bundling up in a half dozen layers was an unavoidable fact for months out of the year, but as anyone from Michigan would tell you the minute the snow melted, and the temperature rises to just barely above freezing the coats get put away and you tough it out. Spring was finally coming, and Leigha could swear she could all but taste the sweetness of it flavoring the night air.

Smiling she turned off the road on to Ridge's drive. The house was blazing with lights beckoning her as she parked and turned the ignition off. Grabbing her purse off the seat she walked quickly up the steps, her anticipation already building. Raising her hand to the door Leigha took a deep breath and knocked. Immediately the sound of excited barking echoed throughout the big house. She heard Ridge talking to Boomer as he approached the door, and the dog sounded like he was tripping over himself to get there first. Leigha was laughing at the cacophony inside when Ridge finally opened the door. Boomer raced out to greet her, and she reached down immediately to pet him. He licked her hand enthusiastically and she laughed some more.

Finally able to look up, the hello she planned on saying got stuck in her throat. He was staring down at her with his lopsided grin and wonder swimming in his forest eyes. Unable to help herself she leaned into him and cupped his cheek in her hand. Ridge leaned into her touch, the smile fading from his face. He wrapped his arms around her, and instead of pulling her into the hug she expected he ran them up her back and straight into her dark brown hair. Using his grip on her hair he tilted her head back and ravaged her mouth with so much hunger it had her offering up everything she had inside. One hand stayed fisted in her hair, but the other one slid slowly back down until it was cupping her ass, and he pulled her tight against his hips. She could feel his dick already growing hard, and her nipples pebbled in automatic response to the pleasure she knew was coming.

Ridge turned her head to the side, still using his hand in her hair, and licked along her ear before he whispered huskily, "You're not wearing a bra."

"I know," she said up to the porch ceiling as they stood there in the open door, while Ridge sucked hungrily on her neck.

She was covered in goosebumps, and it wasn't from the temperature. Wondering if she could get off from just his mouth on her neck alone, she let out a throaty moan. He turned slightly, and Leigha found her back pressed against the door frame as he ground his hips against hers, but it wasn't enough to ease the ache between her legs. Reaching up to his shoulders she wrapped her arms around his neck and brought her legs up. Ridge didn't disappoint her, letting go of her hair and grabbing her legs with both of his hands.

"Inside," he growled into her mouth as he stepped over the threshold into his house. Boomer was still barking, jumping excitedly around him. "Go lay down," he said pulling away from her mouth only long enough to get the words out. Boomer must have listened, because the barking stopped, but Leigha just didn't have it in her right now to bother checking.

Ridge was carrying her somewhere, but as she dug her fingers into his scalp, she realized she would have happily fucked him against the door frame. As he walked, she could feel all his muscles rippling against where she was pressed into him, and she moaned again, into his mouth this time. He let go of her, and she fell a few inches onto a hard, solid surface. He took the purse off her shoulder and set it down. His hands went under her sweater and slid up her heated skin. He cupped her breasts, and squeezed, stopping just this side of pain. Leigha tried to press her thighs together to relieve the pressure knotted there, but Ridge was standing between them. He pulled his mouth from hers and yanked the sweater up over her head quickly. His eyes burned into hers with more heat than she had ever seen in them before, and her tongue slid out to wet her bottom lip. After tossing the sweater somewhere he reached out and rubbed the pad of his thumb over her hard nipple making her shudder. Leigha reached for his shirt and he took a step back pulling it off himself. Leigha sat there on what she now realized was a massive wooden dining room table, and watched his skin come into view. God, but he was absolutely beautiful. She leaned back, pressing her palms against the smooth wooden surface, which she knew he noticed pushed her breasts up invitingly.

His eyes on the tight pink nipples he reached out and unsnapped her jeans, giving them a yank letting her know what he needed. Leigha boosted her hips up helping him take them off her. Once they were clear of her ass he dragged the material slowly the rest of the way down her legs. Wearing nothing but a bright pink lacy thong the table was cold against her skin, adding another sensation into the swirling mix. Ridge ran his hands up her thighs, pulling them even further apart so he could look at everything the lace wasn't bothering to hide from his view.

"Stunning," he whispered roughly, dropping

down to his knees in front of her.

Leaning in, he licked the side of her knee, his tongue making indecipherable patterns against her skin as he headed towards her center. Leigha held her breath in anticipation as she watched him. Instead of going where she needed though he slid right past her lace covered pussy, and bit down on the skin of her other thigh. Leigha's head fell back on a gasp at the delicious sting of his teeth. He licked the spot he bit slowly, to soothe the beautiful ache. Ridge slid his hands up her legs, his fingers calloused from so many years playing the guitar, scraping gloriously across her sensitive skin. Her breathing quickened as he gripped the pink frothy material at each hip and gave a quick yank of his wrists. The material snapped, and he pulled it slowly away from her.

Sitting up straight she reached for his pants, intent on getting him naked too. Ridge caught her hands before she got them undone, and set them back down at her sides. "Not yet baby," he said, his deep voice filled with sexy gravel. He leaned down and licked one of her nipples, pulling the bud into his mouth and sucking on it hard. Leigha reached up digging her hands into his hair to hold on. After a few moments he turned his head, lavishing attention on her other nipple. By the time he released it from his lips she was sure there was a puddle gathering underneath her on the table. Never in her whole life had she been so turned on, and he hadn't even touched her center yet. Ridge finally reached between her legs, and stroked one finger slowly across her pussy.

"Drenched, completely fucking soaked for me," he said circling her demanding clit.

Leigha couldn't form the words to answer as his finger sped up circling faster and faster. She was so close, she could feel the orgasm gathering deep inside. Her thighs started to tremble, and his finger abruptly left her clit.

Leigha's eyes snapped open. "Ridge!" she cried out in frustration.

"What baby?" he asked her softly.

"I was so damn close," she said.

"Oh, I know," he said with a mischievous smirk. "Don't worry Leigha, I'm not in any hurry."

This was something new, they had teased each other before, of course. But this went past teasing straight into seduction, and it was the hottest thing Leigha had ever felt. His eyes were on her face watching her as he pushed a finger up inside her pussy, and withdrew it slowly. She bucked her hips, trying to ride his hand, but he used his other arm and held those eager hips firmly in place. All she could do was open her legs wider, and moan as he took his time. Even with his finger's incredibly slow pace she started trembling again, her breath coming in whimpering gasps. He withdrew his finger from her pussy, and Leigha cried out again.

"Please, Ridge! I need to come." Her whole body was gathered up tight, waiting to leap across the finish line.

Ridge stood up, and with his hands on her hips pulled her towards him. Her ass was hanging partially off the table as he pushed her legs up to balance it out. He stood there staring down at her, the heat in his eyes all but burning her already heated skin. She watched him unbutton his pants, his dick bobbing out as he shoved them down his hips. Leigha licked her lips at the sight of him. He wrapped his fingers around himself, and as she watched he pumped his dick twice. A moan slipped past Leigha's lips, as if he was touching her skin instead of his own. Still gripping his dick, he took a step towards her, and she felt the thick head of him pressing against her. Using his hand, he moved his dick across her clit coating himself in her sweet slickness. Just when she was about to beg him again he jerked his hips forward, finally sliding inside her aching empty pussy.

Leigha let out a thankful cry at his fullness inside of her, and reached out her arms to wrap them around him. Shaking his head he pressed a hand to her shoulder. Leigha laid back, her spine pressing into the unyielding wood. He held her legs open with his hands and pushed into her harder and faster. Leigha's back arched up toward him, and he stopped moving, his eyes on her expectantly. It took her a second to realize why he had stopped and laid back down flat on the table. She was rewarded by his dick sliding into her once more. Figuring out she had to stay like this to keep him powering into her she smiled. This was a new side of Ridge, and it was really working for her. He was pounding into her so hard that she could feel his balls swinging up hitting her ass where it still hung off the table, with each thrust. Every single nerve ending in her body felt like it was connected to a live wire, and the sounds bubbling up from her throat sounded more animal than human.

Nothing had ever felt this good to her before, nothing. He quickened his already punishing pace, and Leigha's whole body started trembling. The orgasm building inside of her right now was bigger than anything she had ever come close to feeling. Digging her fingers into the edge of the table she came with a guttural scream, her pussy gripping him manically as the orgasm coursed near violently through her. Ridge was growling, his strokes getting sloppy, and before she was even done pulsing he was twitching. Shoving his hips forward once more, he stilled deep inside of her with a shout. She watched his face as he came, and he looked every bit as primitive as the way she was feeling inside.

He pulled out of her slowly, making her moan at the emptiness, before he held a hand out to her. Leigha let him pull her off the table. Before her feet could even touch the floor he was picking her up and carrying her up the stairs.

"Did I hurt you?" he asked as he walked.

"That was the best sex I've ever had. What the hell was that?" she asked into the warm skin of his chest.

"I'm not some eighteen-year-old kid Leigha, I couldn't hold back anymore," Ridge said with a laugh, the sound rumbling through his chest.

"Well thank God for that," Leigha said and meaning it with every single cell still vibrating in her body.

Chapter Nine

Ridge reached down and pulled the covers back on his bed, setting Leigha down on top of the sheet. He crawled in next to her and covered them both up. They laid there warm underneath the covers in his bed for a little while. Leigha could still feel the pleasant echoes of Ridge all over her body. A satisfied smile was etched on her face, and she turned to look over at where Ridge was laying beside her propped up on the pillows. He had one muscular arm tucked behind his head, and he was staring down at her. His brown hair was a shaggy mess all over the place. There was an intensity still raging in his green eyes that had a delicious shiver trailing down her spine. Those were not the eyes of a man finished with her for the night, in fact he looked like he was just getting started.

Leigha ran her hand along the planes of his abs, up the mounded pecks and around his neck pressing herself against him as she did. Bringing her mouth up to his she kissed him slowly, savoring the heat she could still taste there. Nope, this definitely wasn't the same eighteen-year-old boy anymore. He hadn't been able to go more than one round at a time back then. As she pulled her mouth away he caught the back of her head and held her there as he had a habit of doing.

"I'm nowhere near finished with you tonight Leigha," Ridge whispered against her lips before his tongue licked the corner of her mouth.

"Mmmm, that sounds good to me," she said huskily. The things he was doing to her body were so damn good.

"How many orgasms do you think it will take to keep you here with me all night?" he asked as he grabbed a handful of her ass and squeezed.

"I can't stay Ridge. That wouldn't be keeping things casual," Leigha reminded him, trying to convince herself just as much as him.

"And we can't have that." Ridge lifted his leg between hers, pressing against all her wet heat.

"We agreed," Leigha moaned.

"No, Sugar, I didn't agree to shit," Ridge said nibbling the sensitive skin just under her jaw.

"But, I thought..." Leigha sputtered, trying to keep her thoughts in line which wasn't very easy with what he was doing to her. Hearing him call her by the old nickname he used when they were teenagers wasn't helping any either.

"It was my only in, and I'm not above using it. I want you back in my life, as more than just someone to warm my bed when you're hungry to get some. But, if I have to convince you to stick around with multiple orgasms, then it's really no hardship. Especially after the way you exploded around me. I've missed you, nobody tastes as sweet as you do Leigha. I was right all those years ago calling you my Sugar." Ridge used the hand on her ass to move her against his leg, teasing her. "Tell me that it's been this good for you with another man." He looked into her eyes, nodding his head. "You can't without lying, because nobody has ever fucked you so good. Even before I knew what the hell I was doing it was better than everyone else you let in after, wasn't it?"

The pressure was already building, just from moving against his leg, and Leigha started to tremble. The things he could do to her body amazed her. He didn't have to move her anymore, she was bucking her hips eagerly against him all on her own. When she didn't answer his question, he gripped her hips, stilling their frantic movement. When she whimpered and tried to move anyway his fingers only dug in holding her immobile. He cocked one dark eyebrow up questioningly at her. Sighing in frustration she admitted, "No comparison. When I

Cara Roman

did have sex, it was never worth it."

"How long?" Ridge asked, back to licking her neck. His tongue making lazy patterns against her skin.

"How long what?" Leigha answered in confusion, her brain not firing on all cylinders with her body still straining for that orgasm.

"How long since you had a man?"

"Until you? A few years, it wasn't worth it. I can do it better myself," Leigha said. Ridge released his hold on her, and she rocked greedily against him.

"Holy shit," Ridge said, his voice rumbling against her skin, in that sensitive spot where her neck and shoulder meet. "C'mon, Sugar," he said as her breath started coming in desperate pants as she got closer and closer. "You like riding my leg dontcha? Well, c'mon then girl, I'm all yours. Work that hungry little pussy on me. Take what you want."

Leigha was too far gone to answer him, and the dirty words spewing from his mouth were only spurring her on. She didn't even know how much she wanted that until now. Digging her nails hard into his shoulders, with a scream she stilled against him, her pussy pulsing against his thigh. Before the pulsing even stopped Ridge was yanking her up, and she found herself eye to eye with his big rustic headboard as he held her to his face. His mouth worked her dragging the aftershocks out. Grabbing onto the wood she held on tight as he sucked her clit into his mouth, and her back arched with the intensity of it.

"I can't Ridge, it's too much," Leigha moaned shakily. He was relentlessly pushing her to another orgasm, and the last one was barely over.

"Yes you can Sugar, I'm not stopping until you don't even know your own name anymore," Ridge said, his breath tickling against her folds.

Leigha started trembling, her whole body shaking with the sensations rampaging through her. Closing her eyes, she let out a strangled sounding scream as she came against his face, the orgasm ripping through her body leaving nothing unscathed as it reached its apex. Ridge licked her slowly while she tried to remember how to breathe. Leigha was glad he was holding her up, because she wouldn't be able to stay upright at that moment if her life depended on it. He eased her down his body until his lips found hers. She reveled in her taste still coating those lips, as she licked them.

"That's right, lick all that sugar, you sure do taste amazing. I don't mind sharing it with you," Ridge said against her lips.

Instead of being embarrassed by the brazenness, she moaned into his mouth and kissed him. Laying on top of his expansively sexy body Leigha could feel how hard his dick was pressed between them. Wiggling herself against it she started sliding down lower. His hands skimmed the skin of her back as she moved down his body. Taking her time to explore the secrets of his skin as she went, by the time she was face to face with his dick her mouth was practically watering for it. Looking back up his body she met his eyes. They were full of enough dark hunger her toes wanted to curl. Opening her mouth she ran her tongue around the swollen head, catching the drop of moisture beading there at the tip. Anchoring herself with her hands on his thighs she sank her head down, taking as much of him into her mouth as she could fit. His hands caught her hair, but instead of guiding the rhythm like she expected him to, he just held it tightly. Her eyes never leaving his she took a breath in through her nose, and moved her head back down. This time when he reached the back of her throat instead of stopping she swallowed, taking even more of him. Moving back up slowly she let the spit pool in her mouth, and with another deep breath and slow descent she worked him against the back of her throat.

Ridge had his bottom lip stuck between his teeth, and she could see his chest rising and falling rapidly as she deep throated his dick. Expecting he would get off soon she was surprised when he let go of her hair grabbed her hips, lifting and turning her around instead.

"Don't want to come down your throat, even as fucking good as that felt. When did you learn to do that?" Ridge said climbing up onto his knees behind her.

Turning her head she looked over her shoulder at him, with a saucy, "I'm not the same eighteen-year-old you left behind either Ridge," she used his own words back on him. Then she leaned down slowly tipping her ass up invitingly for him.

Ridge wasn't the kind of man to waste time, and as soon as the thick head of his dick found her pussy he surged inside. Ducking her head Leigha gasped at how full he filled her from this angle. He stayed fully inside of her not moving and let the tension build. Unable to take it any longer Leigha rocked back and forth, moving herself against him.

"That's right baby, fuck," Ridge growled out, grabbing her hips.

He kept still and let her work him like that for

a few minutes, but no matter how hard she pushed back into him it wasn't enough. Leigha whimpered out her frustration.

"Need more, Sugar?" Ridge asked.

"Yes!" Leigha moaned.

"Tell me, I wanna hear you say it. What do you want me to do to you Leigha?" Ridge asked.

"Fuck me!" she yelled out.

Ridge reached down grabbing a handful of her thick hair, lifting her head up as he grabbed her hip with his other hand. Holding her in place he slammed his hips into her quickly, over and over again. With every breath Leigha was crying out. Her body was on fire, the heat burning through her increasing with every slam of his dick inside of her. Even over her screams she could hear their bodies slapping together. She had never felt more powerful as a woman in her whole life. Being devoured like this, without any wishy-washy manners. Ridge fucked Leigha like a man who knew exactly how much she needed it, and was the only one who would ever be able to give it to her. This was primal, and unapologetic. Gripping the blankets underneath her hands she felt the orgasm tear through her on a trajectory straight into him. As soon as Leigha's pussy gripped down on his dick he slammed into her with a loud growl, his heat filling her.

Leigha's whole body felt boneless, like her skeleton was replaced with Jell-o. Before she could collapse face first at the end of the bed Ridge caught her and pulled her up to the pillows. Her heartbeat still racing she said, "That was..."

"Everything you needed, yeah me too Sugar," Ridge said.

Leigha smiled over at him as her eyes drifted slowly closed. All the intense orgasms blanketing her brain in a sleepy sated fog. She was asleep within moments, and never even felt him get up to let Boomer out one last time for the night. Ridge came back upstairs with her clothes and set them on the chair in the corner of his room before crawling into bed next to her. In her satisfied sleep she didn't hesitate to curl around him as soon as he laid down. Smiling up at the ceiling Ridge wrapped an arm around Leigha and let himself fall asleep.

Chapter Ten

Leigha opened her eyes slowly, and for a few heartbeats she thought she was in her own bed at home. Then the warmth pressed up against her side filtered through, and she realized that she had fallen asleep in Ridge's bed. Spending the night all curled up in his arms like a legitimate couple really wasn't in her plans. In fact, it was the last thing she wanted at the moment. Especially considering how good he felt next to her. This was definitely not keeping it casual, strictly just for sex. Over-nighters were venturing into some very dangerous territory. Leigha sat up, and the sheet slipped down, the cold air making her nipples pucker and reminding her that they did the *get naked dance* downstairs. Sliding out of the bed Leigha made to sneak downstairs, but a cloud moved away from the moon and the room was bathed in a luminous silver glow coming through the large windows. She saw her clothes in the chair, and tip toeing over to the corner she quietly started putting them on. She started the night without a bra, and now she was heading home without panties too. Leigha smiled, remembering the sound her panties had made when Ridge tore them in his rush to get to her. She loved every minute of that, even if she was running away now. So focused on inching the door open wide enough to squeeze through, Leigha didn't notice Ridge sit up in bed.

"Not even gonna say goodbye to me? Well, that's a fine way to treat the man that rocked your world not too very long ago." His voice rumbled sleepily, even more deep and rich than usual.

Leigha could feel it skim across her skin, making her knees weak, and her resolve ready to crumble. Shoring up her spine she said, "I didn't want to wake you." Leigha didn't turn around, she just knew that looking at him right now would be a bad idea, and rob her of the desire to leave.

"Oh, I'm sure you didn't, Sugar. Makes it that much harder to run away." Ridge gave a jaded laugh.

"We're not together Ridge," Leigha said as she pulled the door all the way open now, no need for covert actions anymore. He was right, she was running away, and there was no way for her to deny it.

"If you say so."

He said it quietly, but she still heard him. There was nothing to say to that, nothing she could say to it that made any sense anyway. So she just shook her head and walked out of his bedroom. Boomer met her at the bottom of the stairs looking sleepy and a bit confused. She bent down to love on him a second, before walking across the room for her purse. Pulling the strap up on her shoulder she headed out the front door before she changed her mind. Crossing the dark yard to her car she wondered at why she was even bothering. What would spending the last couple hours before her alarm goes off even matter at this point? Was there really any difference when she already spent hours sleeping curled into his big comfortable frame? Sitting in her car she could admit to herself that there wasn't. They had crossed the line she had drawn already. Leaving was only punishing herself for staying in the first place. Shaking her head at herself she started the car and drove down his driveway.

Back at home Finn was curled up on the foot of her bed sleeping, clearly he listened to her advice and hadn't been waiting up for her. Not bothering to go back to bed since she only had a little while before her alarm she got in the shower. She could still feel Ridge's hands all over her skin, and as she lathered up she smiled thinking of him. He made her body feel things that she didn't even know she needed until he did them. He ruined her heart twelve years ago, and now he was ruining her body too. No other man was ever going to push all the right buttons like he could. They hadn't come close to what he had given her before, so now there really was no chance of it. Even with a decade apart their bodies still wanted the same things. Too bad he couldn't be satisfied with just sex. Now that she knew he wanted more from her there was no way she could continue to sleep with him, no matter how good it was. But damn was it good. Her insides still felt warm and satisfied, and her bones were all but liquefied.

Stepping out and wrapping a towel around her damp skin Leigha skulked into the bedroom. Why did he have to go and ruin a good thing? The sex was phenomenal, that should be enough, right? Her Mom and Dani were both worried about her falling for him again and getting crushed, and instead Ridge was the one wanting more from her. Go figure. Pulling on jeans and a cream-colored waffle knit thermal she walked back into the bathroom. After dealing with all the sex tangles, that no amount of conditioner was able to tackle alone Leigha worked her hair back into a French braid. Picking up her toothbrush she cleaned her teeth, and scowled at herself in the mirror. She was literally glowing, apparently her skin hadn't gotten the memo that she wasn't happy about her night. It actually made her laugh, nearly spitting the toothpaste foam everywhere. Her face was a contradiction with the angry eyes, and rosy cheeks. Spitting carefully into the sink she shook her head at herself.

Out in the kitchen she gave Finn his breakfast. Glancing over at the clock she still had an hour before she needed to leave for work. She popped two pieces of whole wheat bread into the toaster, then slathered enough peanut butter on them that it basically canceled out any attempt at being healthy. Standing at the kitchen counter munching her toast she wondered why she had ever thought anything between her and Ridge would be able to stay simple. They might have off-the-charts chemistry, bodies that were practically made for each other, but their lives were miles—no, worlds—apart.

By the time she walked into Caffeinated Sprinkles she was in a right foul mood. Yanking her apron off the hook she put it on and hastily tied a knot around her waist. Even the smell of coffee beans grinding wasn't enough to chase the annoyance away today. Dani walked in the door, and was almost all the way into the kitchen before she stopped in her tracks and turned to look at Leigha.

"Shit. Come on back and tell me what happened," she said as she shouldered the door open. Her arms full of the boxes containing today's specials. Dani got started on the day's baking in her kitchen at home so she could get Silas up and ready for school before heading in. That was one of the biggest perks of owning the shop, she could arrange her schedule around being a Mom, instead of trying to be a Mom around work.

Leigha huffed out a breath, crossing her arms and walked into the kitchen. "I've got to get the special cookie up on the chalk board Dani."

"Yeah, pretty sure you've got enough time to tell me what's got your panties in such a twist already this morning," Dani said propping her hands on her hips, clearly ready to wait it out.

The two women stared each other down a minute before Leigha caved. "Ridge wants more than just sex," Leigha said like it was completely shocking.

"Of course he does," Dani said.

"What do you mean 'of course he does'?" Leigha stared at her friend.

"You were his first love too, ya know Leigha. He came home needing to feel something familiar again, after his divorce, I'm thinking. There is no way you two could ever just bang and that's it. There is so much water under this bridge, it's a whole damn ocean," Dani said turning around to get to work.

"Well why didn't you tell me that sooner?" Leigha asked begrudgingly.

"Because you wouldn't have listened to me, duh," Dani said the obvious with a shrug.

"That's probably true," Leigha admitted walking over to stand next to her friend, and lean against the big worktable in the center of the kitchen.

"It is," Dani agreed. "So let me get this straight, you're walking around with a near deadly scowl because the man actually wants to be with you?"

"When you say it like that it sounds stupid," Leigha said. Dani just raised an eyebrow and kept silent. "It's not what I want. Ridge isn't the kind of man I need, he's just the one I can't help but want."

"Maybe. Or maybe he has changed more than you're giving him credit for. But you'll never know if you don't actually face what's brewing between the two of you again, instead of ignoring it."

"I don't know if I want to," Leigha said.

"That's your choice, but once you make it, you gotta own it," Dani said wisely.

"Yeah, I know. Thanks Dani," Leigha said bumping her shoulder affectionately into her best friend. "What am I writing on the sign today?"

"Cinnamon roll cupcakes with cream cheese frosting, and white chocolate peanut butter blondies," Dani said carrying the first tray out to the display case. "By the way, nice braid. Haven't seen you wear your hair like that in ages."

Leigha smiled as she followed Dani out. Making sure the special treats were up on the little chalk board Leigha walked over to flip the closed sign over to open. Dani was right, she needed to figure out what she wanted from Ridge, and quickly. He wasn't going to leave her alone for very long. Nobody could say he wasn't a man who went after what he wanted with everything he had. And right now what Ridge wanted was Leigha.

Chapter Eleven

As Leigha pulled into her driveway after work she spotted Ty getting out of his truck. He must have just been getting out of work too. There was a rip in the knee of his jeans, and they looked dirty enough that if he jumped a cloud of dust would rise up into the air around him. He had a flannel open over a gray thermal shirt, with the sleeves rolled up on his forearms. Leigha looked at him and could acknowledge he was basically mouthwatering, but she felt nothing. Her blood didn't sing, goosebumps weren't breaking out along her skin. Her heart didn't thump erratically, and there were no butterflies swarming in her middle. Which was kind of a shame. He started across her front lawn, heading in her direction.

"Shit. Just what I need today," Leigha whispered as she climbed out of her car. "Hey Ty." She pasted on a smile and said as he got close enough to hear her.

"Hey Leigha. Whatcha doin' tonight?" Ty asked smiling. The persistent bugger.

Leigha shrugged trying to think of something

to say when the sound of a truck rumbled up the road. Turning towards the sound she saw Ridge's ride pull over next to her curb. He opened the door and hopped out with a smile on his face.

"Heya, Sugar," Ridge said as he walked over and wrapped his arm around Leigha's waist. "Ty," he said with a nod in his direction.

"Heard you were back Ridge. Been gone a long time now," Ty said, the look on his face was far from friendly.

"Had shit I needed to do. Figured some things out along the way," Ridge bit out, and Leigha felt the tension rolling off him in waves.

"Figured you'd just pick up right where you left off, eh?" Ty asked, his eyes going hard.

"I don't see how that's any of your damn business," Ridge all but growled. He turned to Leigha dipped his face down and asked, "You with him?"

Leigha shook her head slowly from side to side. Feeling both frustrated to be in the middle of this male tug of war, and so turned on by Ridge's possessiveness that her body felt on fire. Damn she was messed up, so much more than she realized.

"Leigha said she's not with you Ty," Ridge said turning back to face him.

"What the hell is that?" Ty said pointing at her. "Is that a hickey on your neck? Fuck, Leigha, he's been in town what, a week now, and he already managed to get you back in his bed. Even after he broke everything you had inside. I might have been away at school, but I saw the empty look in your eyes every time I came home. It took years for them to shine again. And now you're going to give him another shot? You should be with me instead. I would never forget to appreciate you."

Leigha stood there staring at Ty for a full thirty seconds letting it sink in. A hickey, nobody had mentioned it, and she herself hadn't even seen it. Turning to look up at Ridge she raised an eyebrow at him. He smiled down at her, and that was more than answer enough. Stepping out of Ridge's arm she turned back to Ty. "I have told you no over and over, as nice as I could because you're a good man, and I wanted to keep calling you my friend because I like you. But since that's not good enough, let me make this as crystal fucking clear as I can for you. Okay? I will never be with you, no matter how hot you are, oh don't look at me like that, you know you're a catch. We go too far back, and I can't think of you without seeing Ridge. And since you apparently were so tuned into how broken I was before, you should understand that." Ty winced like she had slapped him, and she supposed her words had. Turning to Ridge she said, "And you Ridge, I am a thirty-year-old woman, I am way past the age when walking around with a god forsaken hickey on my neck was cool. I do not appreciate it one bit. Are you actually trying to make me regret fucking you last night?"

Ridge stared at her with an unapologetic smirk on his face through her whole tirade, but she didn't miss the heat burning up his green eyes. "You have no regrets and you know it," he said. "Now that she cleared that up for you, come on by my place for a beer some time Ty." His eyes never left hers even as he spoke to the other man.

"Yeah, sure," Ty muttered before walking dejectedly back over to his house.

"What do you want Ridge?" Leigha said crossing her arms so she wasn't tempted to reach out and touch him.

"You. Always you," he said, and the intensity in his gaze left no argument that he meant exactly what he said.

"Why? You gave me up pretty easily a long time ago," Leigha said.

"You've always meant something to me, this whole time, whether you believe it or not. I won't be giving you up this time, Sugar."

Leigha stood there feeling shell shocked by what Ridge said, and dropped her arms. Never one to miss an opportunity, the moment her arms fell Ridge was pulling her body against his. Her arms wrapped around his neck of their own accord, like so many times before. He watched her eyes as his head came slowly down towards hers. His lips pressed against hers, his tongue licking against her bottom lip demanding entrance. Leigha opened her mouth letting him in, and gave as good as she got. The kiss was a battle of wills, two strong people at war with each other. Ridge wanted Leigha's heart, and she was determined to keep it from him at all costs, even though she couldn't stay away from him.

"Let me in Leigha," Ridge whispered softly against her mouth.

Leigha nodded her head and turned walking to unlock the front door, having never made it into the garage.

"That's not what I meant, and you know it," Ridge said following behind her.

"It's what I can give you Ridge, right now it's all I can give you," Leigha said feeling the warmth of his body melting into her back. Closing her eyes, she took a deep breath and turned the doorknob knowing she just didn't have it in her to tell him to go home. He didn't say anything, but as she stepped over the threshold his hands were on her hips pulling him inside the house with her. Finn meowed in welcome, weaving sinuously through their feet, all but ignored.

Ridge shut the door behind him and turned her around to face him. "Where's your bedroom Leigha?"

She stared up at him a minute, powerless to fight what was happening between them. Reaching out she caught his hand and led the way across the small house to her room. As soon as they were in her bedroom, she shut the door, and shoved him up against it. The heat that started simmering inside of her from his possessiveness in front of Ty was turned up to full on boil now. The satisfied smile on his face as his back met the hard wood was her undoing. Launching at him she was all hands and lips, she couldn't get enough. His shirt went flying across the room, and her fingers dug eagerly into his skin. She was working on his pants when he yanked her own shirt up over her head.

"Hurry," she said as she scraped her teeth along the muscles of his chest.

Ridge didn't say anything, but he made quick

work of her pants. Wrapping her arms around his neck she hopped up, knowing his arms would be there to catch her. His fingers dug into her thighs as he reversed them, and pressed Leigha back into the door. Resting his forehead against hers he pulled his hips away just enough for his dick to slide up inside of her. Leigha closed her eyes on a moan. How could he always feel so damn good? Ridge kept the pace slow for the first few minutes, until Leigha was digging her fingernails into his shoulders needing more.

"Ridge!" she moaned into his mouth.

"Right here Sugar," he said in between kisses.

"Would you move?" she said trying to buck her hips against his. But with his body pressing hers into the door she didn't accomplish much.

"I am. Do you need more?" he asked looking into her eyes.

"God, yes. More, Ridge so much more," Leigha said.

"Remember you asked for it," Ridge said pulling her legs open even further. His hips started moving faster, her ass hitting the door in loud thumps.

He let himself go, his dick pumping into her relentlessly. Leigha threw her head back and cried out loving every savage second of it. The pressure was building deep inside of her center, and she raced furiously towards that feeling, her breath coming in quick gasps. Ridge leaned down, and licked along her neck, and she held him to her with her fingers in his hair. Her body broke around him as she came hard, her legs shaking in his hands. Ridge didn't slow his pace, he just kept powering into her dragging her orgasm endlessly out. Just when she managed to catch her breath another one crashed through her, and she screamed. He pounded her into the door erratically before he stopped, and she felt the warmth of his orgasm shooting up into her pussy.

"I'm not the same dumb eighteen-year-old who left you. I'm going to be the man who never lets you down Leigha. I swear it. Just believe in us," Ridge whispered against her ear.

There was nothing Leigha trusted herself to say to that, so she turned his face and kissed him. Ridge stepped away from the door and carried her across the room to her bed.

Chapter Twelve

Leigha was reeling. Everything inside of her felt like it was spinning out of control in a free fall hurtling towards the ground. Ridge wanted her to believe in him, but she couldn't even believe in her own heart, so how the hell could she trust his? There was no denying how right it felt when she was inside of his arms. The way his body fit perfectly with hers, like they were two pieces of the same whole, and destined to be together. But she had thrown all caution to the wind once and given him every ounce of love she had inside, and he shattered her into millions of lost fragments. Nothing could make her want to feel like that again. The desolate loss of hope crushing her soul slowly one day at a time. Nope. Not happening. And, yet, Leigha wasn't asking Ridge to leave. It felt too damn good being with him, and she was feeling happily drunk on their chemistry.

"Leigha?" Ridge asked hesitantly.

Lifting her head up from his warm chest where she was sprawling she answered, "Yeah?"

"Was Ty telling the truth? Was it like that for

you?" She felt him tugging the end of her braid, pulling the band off. He sifted his fingers through her hair, freeing it.

"Are you asking me if you broke my heart Ridge?" Leigha asked sitting up.

"No, I'm not stupid. I know I hurt you. I'm asking just how bad I broke it," Ridge said surprising her.

Leigha stared down at him, trying to arrange her thoughts into something that would make sense. Ridge laid there against her pillows, waiting. He looked ready to ward off blows, like he knew the answers weren't going to be good. "At first I didn't realize I'd lost you. I was so damn hopeful for your career, and I really believed you would make it. Then each time we talked I felt further and further away from you. We lost us a tiny chunk at a time, which I think is infinitely worse than a clean break. At least that has a chance to heal. I was trying to collect all the lost pieces of my heart for years. By the time you caught the dream you were chasing I wasn't a part of you anymore. But I was still so happy for you. The first time I heard your voice flowing out of the radio I sat down and cried I was so fucking proud. Then you got married, and I stopped trying to put myself back together like I was before, because there was no point. I didn't want to be that woman anymore. I quit the bank job I spent years in college striving for and threw absolutely everything I had into Caffeinated Sprinkles. My work gives me everything I need, and love isn't something that I want anymore," Leigha said as honestly as she could. She laid there breathing for a few minutes feeling her words sink into his soul.

"I pulled over at the border. I sat in my truck staring at the Indiana state line for at least an hour. All I wanted was to turn around and come back to you. But who would I have been then? Another idiot with a dream he was too scared to follow. I could see it all so clearly stretching out in front of me. I would come home, get some job that meant nothing to me, but I would have you, so I wouldn't even care. Until all the what ifs started stacking up around me, turning me into a hard and brittle man. We've all seen guys like that. As much as I wanted to come back to you, I was terrified that one day I would wake up next to you and resent you because I chose you over my dreams. I just couldn't be that man. I just couldn't," Ridge said running his hand over his face.

"I never asked you to choose me over your music Ridge," Leigha said softly.

"I know you didn't, but I almost did." Ridge tugged the ends of her hair. "And it fucking scared the hell out of me."

"That's not what I wanted from you. I knew you were meant for bigger things. I just thought I would be a part of them I guess," Leigha said with a shrug. "But all you talked about on the phone was how Nashville was, and all the cool shit you were doing. You never really asked about me, or school."

"I was lying," Ridge admitted, sitting up.

"What do you mean?" Leigha asked, shocked.

"It was hard Leigha. I was playing anywhere they would let me, and all I ever heard was I was good, but not good enough. I needed more twang, less grit in my voice. I wasn't from down south, so how could I be country enough. Every single day I thought about giving up and coming home. But how could I tell you that? That I felt like a failure, and I knew that I shouldn't have left you. So I made it sound great, hoping you didn't see what a fool I was. I didn't ask how you were because I was too afraid of the answers."

"When you stopped calling me I thought I wasn't enough to compete with that life," Leigha said feeling like the world she knew was slipping away. Thinking back to those phone calls she wondered how she didn't notice he was lying. She was so busy missing him that she wasn't really analyzing what he was saying. It never occurred to her he missed home, simply because he never said it.

"I couldn't afford to pay my cell phone bill and still eat, but I had too damn much pride to admit that to you. Then when things finally started rolling for me, I thought maybe I shouldn't call. I figured that you were probably better without me there. That way you could find some guy that wasn't too busy choosing a career over you. You deserved so much more than me," Ridge said throwing her for yet another loop.

"Are you saying that you were, what, afraid to call me?" Leigha asked, her voice laced with incredulity.

"I'm a selfish bastard Leigha. I didn't want to hear you had moved on, even though I knew you should."

"Move on? I was a complete mess Ridge. I wasn't sleeping, forgetting meals, I'm sure I looked like a zombie at best." Leigha shook her head.

"You've never seen how beautiful you are, even a mess I'm sure half of the campus was dreaming about you being theirs. I was just the first guy to get you in the back of his truck, I didn't get to keep you holding on forever," Ridge said low.

"You weren't just my first, you were everything to me, and you married another woman," Leigha said, the words feeling like they ripped out part of her as they came out.

"Yeah, another one of my mistakes. I've more of them than good choices I think. But it wasn't my biggest though, not by a long shot. Suzy was an easy choice. She was in the business, and we had so many things in common. Our lives were moving parallel to each other's. It made sense in a way, and my manager, publicist, and record label executives fell all over themselves when we hooked up. It looked perfect on paper, added up so nicely. But at the heart of it Suzy and I should have just stayed friends. I never loved her the way I should have, and she deserved to be," Ridge said sighing. "Like I said, I'm a selfish bastard. I've wrecked three lives with my shit choices."

"I don't really know what to say to you right now," Leigha admitted. "I'm going to need some time to process all of that."

"Want me to leave?" Ridge asked leaning in and tucking her hair behind her ear.

His eyes looked so scared she would say yes, because if she did, he would go. With all of the doubt swirling in those gorgeous forest eyes, he looked so much like that eighteen-year-old boy she loved so much. Something had changed between them. Opening her mouth and closing it again, she couldn't make herself say the words asking him to leave even though she knew that she probably should. Shaking her head she tilted her head up for a kiss. He pressed his lips softly against hers briefly. "Hungry?" she asked when his lips left hers, changing the subject. "I've got some steaks we could grill."

"Yeah, I could eat. Steaks sound pretty good." Ridge smiled with obvious relief.

"Baked potatoes, and salad too. I'm all set." Leigha laughed climbing out of bed. "By the way, you don't have to mark your territory with Ty, like I told him, he never had a chance." Walking to her closet she pulled on black leggings, a white tank top, the amazingly comfortable kind with the bra built in, and a long red cardigan. After she was dressed she turned to look at Ridge, he was sitting on the edge of her bed staring at her. His face was all soft, and he had a small smile on his mouth. Going on impulse she walked back over to him and gave his smiling lips a smacking kiss. "Come on, I'm starved," she said and walked out of the bedroom.

They both silently agreed that the deep soul

baring conversation was over for the night. Everything he had said was still floating through her mind, but she refused to dwell on it right now. Ridge commandeered her grill, and she got everything else ready. It felt right having him making dinner with her, and she didn't give a damn that she shouldn't be liking it. Tonight they weren't Ridge and Leigha high school sweethearts still trying to recover from each other. They were just Ridge and Leigha enjoying dinner together, and it was enough.

Chapter Thirteen

Saturday's at their coffee & cookie shop were always a bit hectic. Everyone was stopping in to pick up goodies for the weekend or gathering at the tables to catch up with friends over steaming mugs filled with their choice of personal caffeinated heaven. They were packed from the moment they opened until they closed the doors for the evening, and it was always Leigha's favorite day of the week. Silas usually tagged along with Dani, and today he was sitting at a small two top table with a hot cocoa, cookie, and a video game in hand. He would look up every time the bell dinged announcing new people coming in, waving at everyone he knew, and in a town this small he knew basically everyone.

Tina was filling orders today while Leigha ran the cash register, mainly so she could keep a watchful eye on Silas, but Tina was also asking for more responsibilities, and trying to learn every aspect of Caffeinated Sprinkles. Leigha was quite impressed, and Dani mentioned she thought it might lead to Leigha being able to take a day off now and again. Leigha just laughed considering Dani never took days off either. But it brought up a good point, they were doing well enough now that maybe adding another baker might free Dani up some too. Leigha was mulling all the options over in her mind, turning them this way and that looking for flaws when she heard the excited gasp from Tina next to her. Knowing exactly what that meant she looked up and saw Ridge striding across the shop, nodding his head in friendly greeting here and there at people as he passed by them.

"Hey Sugar," he said with that smirk she adored, as he stepped up to the counter.

"Hi Ridge." Leigha couldn't help but smile back at him. "What would you like today?" she asked.

"Mmmm well that's kind of a hard question to answer right here. But let's just start with a large coffee, black." His voice was filled with charm, and promises for later. Leigha felt a delicious shiver creep down her spine just thinking about it. "Is that Dani's boy?" he asked with a tilt of his head over in the boy's direction.

"Yeah, that's Silas," Leigha answered. "He usually spends Saturdays with us."

"Mind if I pop into the back for a moment, I'd like a word with Dani?" Ridge asked.

"No, go on ahead," Leigha said confused. Ridge walked around the counter and through the door into the kitchen. As tempted as she was to go eavesdrop, there was no way she would do it with all the people around to witness it. That would be pretty damn embarrassing, and start the rumor mill churning fast enough to make her head spin. Ridge wasn't even back there five full minutes, before he walked back out front and around the counter again.

"Can you add a few of whatever those cookies are Silas is munching, enough for the both of us," he added. "Dani said I could keep him company until y'all close in an hour."

He pulled his wallet out of his back pocket, and Leigha took the credit card and swiped it on autopilot, her brain having dissolved to complete mush at how sweet that was of Ridge. Tina was all too happy to hand over his coffee, and grab him some more of Silas's favorite candy chip cookies that Dani made every Saturday specifically for him. Ridge thanked her, and walked over to where Silas sat.

His table was close enough to the counter that Leigha could easily hear everything they said. "Hey, Silas. I'm Ridge, I go way back with your Mom, and I asked if it was cool if I sit with you. I really hate sitting alone, and thought maybe you might help me out?"

Silas looked up at Ridge for a minute, clearly taking his measure as only a child could. His face cleared and he smiled. "Sure, I don't mind, do you know my Auntie Leigha too?"

"Yeah, we all grew up together," Ridge said sitting down in the empty seat. He took a sip of his coffee. After a moment he set the coffee down and handed Silas one of the cookies. The boy sent him a big toothy grin before taking a bite out of it.

"So how come I've never seen you around before Mr. Ridge?" Silas asked.

"Just Ridge, okay?" Ridge said. Silas nodded his head. "I moved away as soon as we all graduated from high school."

"Are you back to visit with all of your old friends? If we ever moved away I think I'd like to come back and see my friends sometimes," Silas said. "But my Dad moved away, and he doesn't come visit," he added quietly.

Leigha wanted to walk over and wrap Silas up in her arms. Just as she moved away from the counter to do that Ridge responded.

"My Dad wasn't around when I was growing up either. It took me a long time to understand that he probably didn't deserve to have me as a son. I'm thinking you're probably a pretty cool guy too, and if your Dad is missing out on all that then he isn't very bright either."

Leigha swallowed hard, and had to fight back tears. Holding her breath, she watched Silas. He nodded his head up and down slowly. "Yeah, he was pretty dumb to let my Mom go too. She makes the best cookies, and she laughs really pretty too," Silas confided in Ridge. "Although she still won't let me get a dog," he added with a shrug.

"Well my dog Boomer loves to make new friends, you should tell your Mom to bring you over sometime and you can play with him," Ridge said laughing.

"You've got a dog? That's so cool! Does he catch tennis balls when you throw them? My friend Charlie's dog does that." Silas beamed.

"Yeah, Boomer'll do that, he'll pretty much play fetch with anything. Tennis balls, sticks, frisbees, you name it," Ridge said taking a big bite out of a cookie.

"Sweet! I'm gonna go ask my Mom if we can come over so I can play with Boomer!" Silas said before jumping up and taking off into the kitchen.

"I think you just got plans for the night, whether you wanted them or not," Leigha called out laughing at Ridge.

"You might be right about that," Ridge said laughing too. Just then Dani walked out of the kitchen being pulled by a very enthusiastic Silas.

"Did you really invite us over to your house tonight to play with your dog?" Dani asked speculatively.

"He sure did," Leigha said before Ridge could get an answer out.

"See, I told you he did Mom," Silas said, clearly insulted his mother had doubted his word.

"We should have dinner over there Mom!" Silas said before turning to Ridge, "Can you cook?"

"I can grill," he laughed. "How do you feel about barbecue chicken?" he asked Silas.

"It's pretty good. Auntie Leigha you should bring some mac and cheese." He turned to Ridge. "It's really good, she puts crunchy stuff on the top, and makes it in the oven. We can make a cake!" He all but shouted with his excitement.

"Well, I wasn't invited," Leigha told Dani.

"Uh-uh. You think I'm going over there without you then you're crazy. You're coming too, I'm roping you in," Dani said wrapping an arm around Leigha with a smile. "How's five o'clock sound?"

"Works for me. Leigha?" Ridge said tossing the question back her way.

"I've gotta grab the stuff for the mac, but yeah five's good," she said looking over at Silas. The excitement was all but pouring off him in tangible waves. There wasn't much she wouldn't do for that boy, and an impromptu dinner party didn't even begin to scratch the surface.

"Well I was going to try and convince you to go for a drive with me after you closed, but now I think I've got to get some chicken marinating," Ridge said leaning over the counter. He reached out and tucked a strand of hair that had escaped her ponytail behind her ear. His voice dipping low enough to make her squirm. "See you later Sugar." The heat in his eyes was unmistakable, and Leigha smiled as she nodded.

After closing at two for the afternoon Leigha ran to the grocery store to pick up what she needed. She also grabbed a bottle of wine on impulse, very careful to not ask herself why she was doing it. At home she spent some time cuddling with Finn on the couch until he walked away with a typical feline flick of his tail. Getting up she made the cheese sauce and after pouring it over the pasta stuck it all in the oven. She cleaned the house up while it cooked. When the timer went off, she melted butter adding it to some breadcrumbs. Pulling the bubbling hot macaroni out of the oven she liberally sprinkled the breadcrumbs over the top, and popped it back in.

Hurrying into her room she pulled off the CS logo t shirt she wore to work that day. Lifting a soft button front shirt in a deep plum from a hanger in her closet she smiled. Pulling her hair out of the ponytail she walked into the bathroom. Turning this way and that to see if the top looked good she nodded her head. It did. She ran her fingers through her hair rearranging the waves, and sprayed on a little perfume. Hearing the timer buzzing she walked back into the kitchen. Pulling the casserole dish out of the oven she bent down grabbing the thermal carrier her Mom had insisted she would need someday for potlucks. Smiling, figuring she owed her Mom a thanks on that one, she loaded up her contribution to the meal.

Leigha pulled up to Ridge's house about ten minutes early and smiled seeing Dani and Silas weren't here yet. Ridge walked out of the house as she was opening the passenger door to grab the food. Handing him the bottle of wine she closed the door and lifted her head for a kiss. A smile sparkling in his green eyes he leaned down and kissed her like they weren't about to be joined by an eight-year-old and his mother for dinner.

Leigha was just setting down the casserole dish on the island in the middle of Ridge's massive kitchen when she heard a car pull in. Ridge grinned at her and walked back out front, Boomer hot on his heels. Leigha followed behind them and made it to the doorway in time to see Silas throw open the back passenger door of Dani's car and be greeted by a very excited Boomer. He was licking Silas, his tail whipping back and forth.

"Silas, Boomer, Boomer, Silas," Ridge said making introductions.

"Hi Boomer, Ridge told me you like to play catch, so Mom and I picked up some new tennis balls at the store on the way over!" Silas said reaching back into the car. "I opened them already." He pulled one out and Boomer immediately sat down in the grass eagerly waiting for the ball to be tossed. Silas took a step away from the car, reached way back and sent the ball sailing into the yard as hard as he could. Boomer gave a happy bark and took off after it.

"Well he is gonna want to be over here all the time now," Dani said with a smile on her face as she pulled a bakery box out of the hatchback.

"He is welcome anytime Dani," Ridge told her taking the box. "You are too ya know," he added.

"You're making it awfully hard to be mad at you for breaking my best friend's heart," Dani said.

"Good. Then my well-crafted plan is working," Ridge said with a wink.

"Sure is. I've missed you Ridge, welcome back," Dani said hugging him around the box. Ridge hugged her back with his free arm.

"Missed you too," he said with a sigh. "Why don't you and Boomer bring the game out back so I can watch all the fun while I'm grilling our chicken?" Ridge called out to Silas. He came running and Boomer followed happily along.

They sat at Ridge's massive dining table and ate grilled barbecue chicken, baked macaroni and cheese, and the salad Leigha tossed together. Silas entertained them all, keeping them laughing throughout the whole meal. After the food was all gone Ridge turned on the outdoor lights and went out back to play with Silas and Boomer. Dani stood next to Leigha by the French doors and watched them.

"It's times like this I wish he had a Dad the most," Dani said softly. "Seeing him running wild, soaking up all the male attention. I'm a good Mom, I do my best, but I just can't be that for him."

"You're a great Mom Dani, the best. Silas told Ridge today that his Dad was pretty dumb to let you two go, and he was right. Jason is missing out on the best damn thing that ever happened in his life. If anyone knows what that's like though, its Ridge," Leigha said.

"That's true, I'd forgotten about Ridge's Dad. I'm even more glad that he decided to make friends with Silas then. He's a good man Leigha, you see that right?" Dani asked.

"I'm starting to," Leigha said nodding her head.

Chapter Fourteen

Leigha stood on the front porch waving goodbye as Dani and Silas headed back home. Ridge started out beside her waving at them too, but as they lost sight of the car through the trees, he wrapped his arm around her and pulled her against his hard body. Leigha sighed knowing she should be fighting it, but they were like magnets constantly drawn together, and the pull was too strong to bother fighting. His hand rested on her hip, fingers rubbing on the soft material of her shirt slightly, and it felt more real than all of the doubts swirling around her head.

"Will you stay with me tonight Leigha? The whole night?" Ridge asked quietly his other hand tucked in his pocket. He didn't say please because it would be too close to begging, but his careful tone told her he was afraid to let her know how much her answer meant to him.

Leigha watched the reflective collar glowing as Boomer ran around the yard doing his business in the dark before trotting happily back up the steps to them. It was obvious he had enjoyed all of the fetch and fun earlier.

"My bag's in the car," Leigha finally admitted with a sigh.

"Bag?" Ridge asked with an edge of hope creeping into his voice.

"With clothes for tomorrow," Leigha said. "I don't know what's happening between us, but I know I get one day completely free each week, and I really want to spend it with you. I don't want to deny myself that, it just feels like a waste of time."

"So you're telling me that I get you all night long, and tomorrow too?" Ridge asked walking them inside the house, the happiness ringing in every word.

"Unless you don't want me," Leigha said with a smile.

"Oh, that's never been a problem. How on earth will we ever fill all that time?" he joked.

"I'm sure you can think of something," Leigha said turning towards him. She bumped against him, and his arms closed around her, holding tight.

Ridge leaned down to whisper in her ear, "Mmmhmmm, and you're gonna love them all." His hot breath tickling her skin.

Leigha shivered in his arms, and he made an appreciative rumbling sound deep in his throat. She loved knowing that he always wanted her just as bad as she wanted him. Their desire each fed the others. Threading her fingers up into his hair she pulled his mouth down to hers, kissing him long and deep. Ridge reached down and picked her up, and she wrapped her legs around his waist as he carried her upstairs. "I forgot to go grab my bag," she mumbled against his mouth.

"Get it later. Much later," he said squeezing her ass to make his point.

Leigha nodded her head before going back to feasting on his mouth. Later was good. At the top of the stairs, he turned towards his bedroom, and walked them inside. Using his foot, he shut the door behind them. Leigha expected her back to hit the door, but instead he walked them over to his bed, and set her on her feet. He reached behind his head and pulled off the forest green long-sleeved t-shirt he had on. She immediately ran her hands up his warm muscled skin. While she explored the planes of his chest he undid his pants and pushed them down. Seeing his hard dick, she ran her hand down the front of his abs eagerly towards it. Ridge stopped her hand just centimeters before it got to its destination.

"Not yet," he said shaking his head before slowly unbuttoning her shirt. He took his time, and with each new button freed of its hole her desire grew. When he finally slid the shirt off her shoulders and down her arms, her breath caught in her throat. He moved on to her jeans next, and pushed them down her hips slowly going down on his knees to help her step out of them. He traced his hands up her legs as he stood up. Hands on her hips he backed up a step and let his eyes roam all over her body. She could almost feel their touch across her skin, and reveled that he could make her heart pound with just his eyes. He always looked at her like had had never seen her skin before, and she loved it. The air was thick, the need swirling between them a tangible thing.

"Pink," he said with a gravelly voice.

One side of Leigha's mouth tipped up in a naughty smirk. She'd known the bright pink bra and panties would get to him when she put them on. He always did love her in that color. Some men liked red, but whenever she had pink lace on the fire in Ridge's eyes had burned even hotter. The ones he had ripped off her the other day were pink too. Holding her arms out to the sides she turned a slow circle for him, keeping eye contact over her shoulder as long as she could. "Just for you," she said when she finally faced him again.

Ridge licked his lips, and nodded his head. The muscle in his jaw was ticking deliciously, and she knew he was holding himself back. She reached an arm behind herself and undid the clasp on her bra, holding it to her with the other arm. She waited until she saw his hands clench into tight fists before letting the frothy lace fall away from her breasts. His dick gave a quick jerk upwards, and she wanted him so much more because he had never shied away from showing her everything she did to him. But she was enjoying this slow burn, so she inched her hands down her own body, tracing all the skin his eyes had devoured. When she finally reached the lace riding on her hips she hooked her thumbs in and turning around pulled them over the globes of her ass, and bent at the waist to ease them down her legs, giving him an eye full of her pussy in the process. Standing slowly back up she turned back to face him.

"Come here," he said low. "Now."

Leigha stepped up to him, wrapping her arms around his neck. Tipping her head up she waited for his kiss. Sliding one arm around her, he gripped her hair and he leaned his head down to kissed her mouth hungrily. His dick pressed against her stomach, and she swiveled her hips, rubbing it against her skin. With their height difference it wasn't where she wanted it, but she liked teasing him anyway. Ridge sat down on the bed and scooted up against the headboard. He raised an eyebrow and tipped his head back, inviting her up. She smiled and leaned down on her hands, sliding slowly up his body. They hadn't touched each other much at all, but she was already dripping wet, and craving him desperately. Leigha's fingers dove into his messy dark hair as she lifted onto her knees, straddling his waist.

"I've never wanted another woman the way I want you," he confessed.

Leigha froze on top of him, his clear green eyes blinking up at her, his lips parted slightly in anticipation and she nodded her head. She knew exactly what he meant. It was obvious he couldn't get enough of her either. Her eyes never leaving his she sank slowly down on to his waiting dick. She bit her lip, taking a moment to absorb how good he felt filling her pussy like that. She never got sick of how he felt inside of her. He didn't rush her, he just waited perched on the edge of desire with her. Lost in the beauty of his eyes, and his heart that she couldn't help but see shining up through them she finally moved her hips. She had intended to go slowly, continuing the teasing pace they had been on, but she needed him too badly all of a sudden. Ridge gasped as she bobbed up and down just as quickly as she could, surprising him with the force of her need too. The momentum had her breasts bouncing and he reached out and finally touched them. Holding them in his hands he pinched her nipples, and a long moan left her throat at the contact. She gripped his hair, riding him even harder.

"Jesus, Sugar," he groaned.

"Need you so bad Ridge," she whimpered. The intense pressure building inside of her.

"I'm all yours, take what you need," he said one hand reaching around to tangle into her hair as it moved across the skin of her back. He gave it a quick tug and she moaned, her hips whipping up and down.

She felt his hands gripping her hips, fingers digging in. The closer she got to the orgasm the bigger it grew, just out of her reach. Growling in frustration Leigha grabbed the wood of the headboard behind his head and used it to pull herself towards him on every downward stroke. "Yes. Yes. Yes!" she chanted. Staring down into his eyes she shuddered, the massive orgasm shooting through her body. Crying out she stilled, unable to move with the force of pleasure pulsing through her. Ridge watched her a heartbeat, bottom lip between his teeth, feeling her quaking around him, before he used his hands on her hips to lift her as he pounded up into her. Leigha was just coming down from her orgasm, and gasped as he pushed her into another one. Tipping her head back she screamed up at the ceiling, her body gripped in another shattering orgasm. So lost in the way her own body felt she didn't even notice he was close until he stopped moving. His dick jerked in time to the pulsing waves inside of her pussy as he filled it with the familiar warmth.

After their hearts finally stopped thundering Ridge threw on his pants and went down to get her bag out of the car. He took longer than Leigha expected, and she was just about to wander down and see what was going on when he walked back into the room. Her bag caught in the crook of his elbow, the bottle of wine she bought earlier in hand, and two wine glasses clasped in the other. He was smirking as he set her bag on the chair in the corner of his bedroom, and walked over to her. The wine was already opened, he set the glasses on the nightstand and poured the dark red liquid into them. Smiling from ear to ear, Leigha scooted over to make room for Ridge, and he got into bed beside her then picked up the glasses, handing one over to her.

They slowly worked their way through the whole bottle of red, talking and laughing about old memories long into the night. Ridge set their glasses next to the empty bottle, and turned out the light. They made mad love again, always desperate for each other, in the dim room lit only by the silvery moon before falling into a satisfied sleep, their warm bodies tangled around each other.

Chapter Fifteen

The scratching on the bedroom door woke Leigha up the next morning, and glancing over at the digital alarm clock perched on the nightstand she groaned. It was technically still morning, but only barely. Ridge was still asleep in the bed next to her, so she eased out from underneath the covers slowly. Picking up the first item of clothing she came across, which was one of his flannel shirts, and it thankfully covered her all the way down to her thighs, she walked to the door. As soon as she pulled it open Boomer gave a soft but urgent sounding woof, and took off down the stairs like a shot. Leigha found him waiting by the back door, all but vibrating with his need to be let out to do his necessary business. The cool air kissed the skin of her bare legs as she stood in the doorway watching the beautiful chocolate lab run around the yard, peeing rather enthusiastically in several different spots. She was laughing, caught up in his silliness and didn't notice Ridge walk up behind her.

"You look better in my shirt than I do, baby." His voice was still delectably raspy and rough from sleep.

Leigha took a deep breath of the crisp air, admitting to herself that the chills that just went down her spine had nothing at all to do with the air outside. It was just Ridge. Her body always responded to his on a purely elemental level, and there was never anything she could do to stop it. "Boomer really needed to go out," she said looking over her shoulder at him. He had slipped on a pair of boxer shorts before heading down, but that's not what she noticed. His face looked softer from sleep still, reminding her of how he had looked before he took off for Nashville. Her heart thudded erratically inside her chest and her mouth went bone dry. This was happening again, her heart desperately wanted to leap out of her body and land at his feet. Grabbing onto the door frame to keep herself locked in place Leigha tried to patch up all the cracks splintering the walls she worked so damn hard to keep up around her heart.

Ridge didn't seem to notice the internal battle she was waging with her own heart, and he walked over kissing her temple gently. "You don't have to stand in the doorway freezing, Boomer knows not to leave the yard. Thanks for letting him out for me Sugar." He walked away into the kitchen. "How about I make us some pancakes? I've even got blueberry syrup," he added with a wink, remembering her fondness for the topping.

"Sounds great," she said, stepping inside and closing the door.

Walking slowly over to the breakfast bar and sitting down on one of the stools. Leigha was having a hard time forming words, thankfully Ridge didn't seem to need any. He wandered around the kitchen pulling the things he needed out of cabinets and drawers. He was humming, and Leigha doubted he knew that he was doing it. She didn't recognize the song though. He used to do that sometimes before, a smile on her face Leigha remembered the time he got detention when he wouldn't stop humming in English class. He tried to tell their teacher he wasn't trying to, it just happened sometimes. But Mr. Pratchett hadn't believed him, having already decided that Ridge was purposefully being annoying.

Things like that kept weakening Leigha's resolve. All the good memories were starting to overtake the hurt that came after. Ones she had forgotten about, or refused to think of, kept slipping in when she least expected it. He was winning this fight for her heart, and he didn't even have to do anything. All the millions of little things that had made her love him so much back then, were the same things she tried so hard to forget all these years. Leigha could almost see the present overlaying the past, like a thin sheet of paper. As if she could trace what she wanted to on it, and leave out all the parts that she didn't.

Arms on the counter, chin in her hand, Leigha watched Ridge turning sizzling bacon in a frying pan, before pouring the pancake batter onto a griddle. The muscles in his bare back rippled with his movement, and she sighed in pure female appreciation. If men knew how sexy women found it to watch them cook, they would all do it a hell of a lot more often, that's for sure. Leigha was thinking that maybe after breakfast, scratch that, brunch considering the time, she could talk him into fucking her brains out on the counter. Boomer barked at the back door to be let in, interrupting her torrid fantasy. Scooting off the stool she walked over to let the dog in so Ridge could keep cooking their meal. Boomer walked in and right over to his water dish, lapping it up thirstily before wandering out to the living room.

"Do you need to get home to feed Finn?" Ridge asked as he set strips of crispy bacon on a plate lined with paper towel to absorb excess grease.

"He should be alright for the day. I made sure he has enough before heading over," Leigha said thinking it was nice of him to think about her cat. "Cats do much better hanging out on their own than dogs do I think," she said sitting back on the stool.

Ridge nodded his head, and turned back to flip a pancake. "Do you want some coffee?"

"No, I don't usually drink it when I sleep in so late," Leigha answered laughing. "Don't tell anyone that though. It might be bad for my business."

"Me either, and don't worry your secrets are always safe with me." He smiled.

Ridge set two plates loaded with delicious smelling food on the bar, one in front of her and the other next to her. Turning away he reached into the refrigerator and pulled out a carton of orange juice, and poured them each a glass. Walking back over to the counter next to the stove he grabbed the two bottles of syrup, one traditional maple, and the other the promised blueberry flavor. She knew he didn't like it, so he had bought it to keep here just for her. Leigha waited until he was seated next to her, and had a chance to take a few bites of his food before she asked, "How long have you had Boomer?"

Ridge glanced over at her, but finished chewing the food in his mouth before answering.

"I've had him for three years, but the shelter said he was around a year old when I got him."

"He's a rescue?" Leigha said surprised, and admittedly impressed. Ridge could definitely afford to pick out the fanciest puppy from any of the most prestigious breeders in the country if he wanted to.

"Yeah, it gets hard being on tour all alone. I mean, you're not exactly alone, but it feels that way. I figured a dog might chase some of that loneliness away, especially one that needed me as much as I needed him," he said in between bites.

"But you were married," Leigha said completely confused.

"Yeah, Suzy had her own career though. She was on the road just as often as I was. We only did one short tour together, just after we got married. We didn't spend as much time together as you're probably thinking, and honestly some of the loneliest times of my life were laying in bed at night with her sleeping next to me. That is a horrible thing to admit, but I told you before that we never should've gotten married. I used to lay there staring up at the dark ceiling wondering what you were doing, then hating myself for it," Ridge said. "I guess I wasn't a very good husband, thinking about another woman while I was in bed with the one I'd said vows to."

His candor surprised her. Focusing on eating for a few minutes, she let her mind run ahead. Most of the divorced people she knew tended to blame each other, instead of seeing their own mistakes. "That must have been hard on the both of you," Leigha finally said quietly.

"It had its moments, that's for damn sure. In the end it seemed like our split broke everyone's heart but mine. That was the most fucked up part. My publicist damn near had a coronary when she found out. She actually suggested we stay married for our careers, and just see other people secretly." The harsh edge to his voice told Leigha exactly what he thought of that.

"I can't even imagine having that many other people feel like they get a say in my life," Leigha admitted. "Sure, I've got my parents and Dani, but they love me, ya know. If something didn't make me happy, they wouldn't want me to continue it for their own selfish reasons."

"Yeah, that definitely makes a difference. Ma wasn't very happy I married Suzy in the first place though. Liked her plenty, she's a hard woman not to like, but said she wasn't meant for me. Of course I didn't listen to her, but she didn't harp on it. Told me once, then let me make my own mistakes."

"I always did like her, how is Diana doing these days?" Leigha said, not wanting to hear more about the intricacies in Ridge's relationship with his ex-wife right now.

"She's great. I fly her out to shows every so often, and she proudly wears one of the official tour t-shirts telling any and everyone who will listen that she's my Ma," Ridge laughed.

"I can see her doing that. She must be so damn proud of you she's nearly bursting," Leigha said laying her hand on top of his. "I know you always wanted to take care of her."

"It's rough being a single Mom. She never complained about having to raise me on her own though. I'm proud to be able to pay her back for everything she did for me," Ridge said giving her hand a squeeze before getting off the stool and taking his plate to the sink. "So, I was thinking we could go for a drive today. How's that sound Sugar?" Ridge asked with a devastatingly handsome smile on his face.

"Where to?" Leigha asked carrying her plate over to the sink and leaning against his warmth.

"Somewhere we can get some mud on my tires," Ridge said wrapping his arms around her.

"The trails," Leigha said thinking back to all

the times she sat next to him as they bounced and rumbled along the little two tracks through the woods. Reaching up she twined her arms around his neck and smiled. "Perfect." Then she reached up on her tippy toes to kiss his lips. He tasted like the food they shared, but like always he just tasted like Ridge, and she was coming to understand that meant home to her.

Ridge leaned into her body, pressing it against the cabinets behind her. The edge of the hard granite countertop biting into the top of her ass. Moaning into his mouth Leigha pulled him even closer. With a teasing nibble he pulled back from her lips. Staring down into her eyes he undid the buttons of his flannel shirt that she had on. Parting the material, he sucked in a hissing breath, and Leigha felt the sound like a kick to her blood stream. Reaching her hand down into his boxers she found him already rock hard. Wrapping her fingers around his dick she stroked it. "All I could think about while you were cooking was how badly I wanted you to fuck me here in your fancy kitchen," she said, her voice husky with need.

"Oh yeah? Well, I aim to please," Ridge said grabbing her hips and boosting her up onto the counter.

Leigha still had her hand in his boxers, but Ridge was holding her wrist keeping it still. His head dipped down and he licked a trail from the base of her neck across the top of her full breast, to her pink nipple. He circled his tongue softly around the peak, and she closed her eyes on a moan. Everything he did to her always felt so good. Leigha cried out when his teeth tugged on it. Reaching up she grabbed his head, weaving her fingers through his hair, needing to hold onto him. He looked up, and his eyes met hers as he licked across the valley between her breasts over to the other nipple that was feeling lonely and waiting for his mouth. He swirled his tongue almost lazily around this one too, but Leigha knew better this time, and she watched as he bit down on the tender peak. She felt the jolt straight down into her pussy, and she shuddered with need.

He stood up and shoved his boxer shorts down. His dick popped out, looking deliciously exciting. Leigha wanted her mouth on him bad, but not nearly as bad as she wanted him buried inside of her. Licking her lips thinking that later she was going to take her time with him, getting him off slowly, and swallowing everything he had to give.

Ridge watched her. "A man could get used to his woman looking at his dick like that."

"So, I'm your woman now?" Leigha said. Partly to tease him, but also hearing him say that had felt good, making her feel the telltale flutter of little butterfly wings inside of her stomach.

Ridge pulled her to the edge of the counter, and she felt the tip of his dick against her entrance. Rocking her hips forward greedily she tried to take him all the way inside. But Ridge moved back denying her what she wanted. "You've always been my woman," he said before sliding slowly into her pussy. Leigha gasped. Ridge didn't move, locked inside of her, while she drenched his fullness. "Say it."

Leigha looked up into his eyes, trying to remember what he wanted her to say. Her mind was a lust filled haze, and she asked, "What?"

"That you're my woman," Ridge said. The words fighting their way out between his clenched teeth as he held the reins on his own need to move.

Leigha tried to move her hips, looking for the friction she needed. Ridge held her still though, with a shake of his head, and she couldn't chase her pleasure. He arched an impatient eyebrow at her. She finally understood that if she wanted him to move, to ease that gnawing ache he needed to hear those words first. "I'm yours Ridge, still yours,"

Leigha whispered.

Ridge growled and finally started moving. They didn't do slow and easy very well, and this time was no different. He was slamming into her so hard that if he weren't holding her hips she wouldn't be able to stay on the edge of the counter. She loved how dominant and commanding he was sexually now. She could let go and trust that he would take care of her body exactly like she needed. There were no boundaries, they went where the need took them. He reached a hand down and pressed his thumb against her clit, and she let out a whimper of encouragement. Her body was flying towards the cliff at breakneck speed. Within seconds her back arched and she let out a long, drawn-out moan as she came.

Ridge groaned, burying his face in the side of her neck. He didn't stop though, his hips kept pumping, relentlessly against hers dragging her from one orgasm straight into another. Her pussy clenching his dick in near violent pulses as the second orgasm ripped through her. Ridge sped up even faster, and Leigha could barely drag air into her lungs. It felt like too much, and not nearly enough at the same time. He wasn't giving her time to come down from one peak before shoving her relentlessly up another one. She felt him growing impossibly bigger inside of her, and knew he was getting close to the edge now too. He swirled the thumb still pressing against her clit, and she screamed breaking apart a third time. This time as she shuddered, he stilled inside of her, coming with a hoarse shout.

Leigha held Ridge as their breathing slowed down. She felt every single nerve ending from the tips of her toes to the roots of her hair singing. This man could do things to her body that even she didn't know were possible, and she loved every single glorious second of it. When Ridge slid out of her and stepped back, he stared into her eyes, and pressed a sweet kiss to her forehead. He stepped away and opened the drawer next to the sink. She watched him pull out a washcloth, turn the water on, and wet it. Walking back over to her he leaned down and cleaned their mingled fluids from her thighs before pulling her gently off the counter and setting her on her feet. Leigha was staring up at him, lost in his eyes, a jumble of feelings clogging up her throat. She opened her mouth to say something she knew she shouldn't, and the shrill sound of a phone ringing broke the silence. And the moment.

"I'm going to grab a quick shower while you answer that," Leigha said gripping the shirt closed as she darted out of the kitchen and up the stairs.

"Damn it," Ridge said with frustration as he watched Leigha escape.

Chapter Sixteen

Ridge was sitting perched on the end of his bed when Leigha walked out of the bathroom after her shower wearing a gray long sleeve cotton shirt, and a pair of dark skinny jeans. When she was packing the bag at home yesterday it seemed like a failsafe choice. Comfortable no matter what they ended up doing, and she knew for a fact that her boobs looked good in the top. The softness she had enjoyed seeing on his face first thing this morning was long gone now though. Replacing it was a hard mask of annoyance that had Leigha realizing that phone call must not have been a very good one.

"What?" she asked, bracing herself for the answer she feared was coming.

"I've got to go back to Nashville today. That was my manager on the phone, and there are some issues with the fucking record label that I'm told can only be handled in person," Ridge said standing up. "I'll only be gone for a few days." She could hear he didn't want to go, but that didn't much matter, he still had to leave. He would always have to leave.

"Oh, okay. Well, that's where the epicenter of

your career is, so really it makes complete sense. Do you need a ride to the airport, no, I'm sure you don't." Shaking her head as she answered her own question. "I'll, ah, get out of your hair so you can take a shower and pack too, you probably need to pack, right? And get Boomer ready to go, he probably has a bunch of stuff you have to get around," Leigha said shoving her things messily into her bag as she rambled. "Have a good flight though," she said heading as quickly as she could towards the bedroom door.

"Sugar." Ridge said reaching his hand out and catching her arm as she passed by. "I'm coming back to you, this is just a quick trip. Downstairs you said you're my woman, and I'm gonna hold you to that." He was staring down into her eyes, the green blazing like summer leaves dappled with sunshine.

Leigha nodded her head slowly, soaking in every single detail of his face. He might be saying he was coming back, but she couldn't afford to believe in that. Leigha reached up cupping his face in her hand, feeling the stubble that he hadn't gotten a chance to shave yet this morning. She knew she heart was swimming in the chocolate depths of her eyes, and she couldn't do a damn thing to hide it. Her eyes always betrayed her. He turned his head, laying a sweet kiss on the center of her palm. Her hand was still zinging from the contact when she pulled it away, and walked out of his bedroom.

She didn't take a breath until she was pulling the driver's side door open. Tossing her bag over into the passenger seat, she quickly hopped in. Her hands were shaking as she put the key in the ignition and started the engine. As it roared to life she glanced up and saw Ridge staring down at her from the window. His face full of angles and hard lines. She pulled out of his driveway and felt every inch of the distance growing between them. Leaving Ridge felt so wrong, but she wasn't really the one leaving, she was just going home before he left. He was the one flying out today. Back to the life that had already stolen him from her once before.

Locking everything inside down, the drive home passed by in a blur. Leigha drove the familiar roads on auto pilot, her knuckles white from holding onto the steering wheel so hard. She hit the button hanging from her visor for her garage before she was even pulling into the driveway. As soon as she shut the car off, she was closing the door behind her. Sitting in her car inside the dimly lit garage Leigha couldn't hold the tears back anymore. They were cruising down her cheeks in a hot rush, and she dropped her head to the wheel in front of her and felt like such a fool. She had always known that he wasn't made for this town. A quick trip back was going to stretch on and on, and he would get too busy to remember to come back. She had lost Ridge once already to the magical draw of Nashville, why should this time be any different.

Leigha knew she shouldn't trust the butterflies dancing in her stomach this morning. They never led anywhere good. Hope was a four-letter word, and she had allowed herself to indulge in it. Stupid, stupid, stupid. Shaking her head, she grabbed her bag off the seat next to her and got out of the car. Her phone buzzed, and she ignored it. There was no point in chasing after something that was already gone. Opening the door, she walked through the house, and straight into her bedroom not bothering to turn any lights on. Flopping down on her bed she stared up at the ceiling wondering how she had let this happen to her again. Finn jumped up on the bed and laid down on her stomach. Reaching her hands up she scratched and petted him. The rumbling sound of his purring filled the room, comforting her.

Disappointed in herself she admitted, "Well I've made a real mess of things now Finn. That man is seriously fucking poisonous to me. No matter how hard I tried to keep him out he managed to sneak in anyway. And I let him. All because I thought it would be okay to have some fun in bed with him for a while. Oh, it was fun to be sure, and toe-curling, god he is the best, nobody does the things to my body he can. But look at me now, huh, crying on my bed. Again, just like twelve years ago. I'm such a damn fool," Leigha whispered to Finn. He didn't answer her, of course, because he was a cat, but he also didn't judge, and talking to him helped.

She lay there on the bed, staring numbly out the window, and doing her best to pretend the outside world didn't exist, as the day slid past. Leigha never got up to check her phone, even though she could hear it buzzing sporadically. Tomorrow was soon enough to face everything. She dozed off shortly after the sun went down, emotionally exhausted from the thoughts whipping through her brain all day.

Chapter Seventeen

In an unsurprising turn of events, Monday morning dawned as usual without any consideration for Leigha's heartbreak. Dragging herself out of bed when her alarm started buzzing Leigha headed into the shower stripping out of the clothes she put on at Ridge's house as she walked. As she stood under the hot spray washing her hair, she wished for the very first time since opening Caffeinated Sprinkles that she could just call in sick. Doing that wouldn't be her though, so she rinsed her hair off and stepped out of the shower determined to face the day. She knew this day was coming eventually, had talked a big game to her Mom and Dani how she could handle it. That while her eyes were wide open, her heart was remaining firmly closed. As she brushed her teeth she wondered if she had been less than honest with them, or just lying to herself the whole time like her Mom thought. Looking in the mirror as she ran the wide tooth comb through her long hair untangling it, she thanked her lucky stars that her eyes weren't all red and puffy after the crying jag last night. If only she had been able to juggle having him while keeping him at a distance.

After pulling on one of her Caffeinated Sprinkles logo shirts, and a pair of jeans that had a rip in the left knee she called it good enough. Shutting the bedroom light off she walked out into the kitchen to feed and water Finn. Her cell phone was still in her purse sitting on the counter where she dropped it yesterday when she got home from Ridge's. Sighing she opened her bag and pulled it out. There were at least a dozen notifications. Her Mom had called her, Dani sent a text, and the rest of them were from Ridge. He had called and texted numerous times.

I know what you're thinking, I'm coming back.
I wouldn't be going if I didn't have to.
I'm heading to the airport now.
I'll let you know when I land.
I made it safe.
Leigha, baby?
Are you OK?
This isn't the end.
I promise you Leigha.
Damn it, I promise!

Leigha stood there at the counter scanning through all the texts. Shaking her head, she sat the phone down and struggled not to let the tears burning her eyes fall. A few deep breaths, and it was under control, the tears locked away. For now. As she was sliding the phone back into her purse another text came buzzing through.

Have a good day at work Sugar.

Leigha powered the phone off and set it on the counter instead of inside her purse. She was not about to hear it buzzing and torturing her all day. There was nothing she had to say to Ridge. Nothing she could say. He was living his life, and so was she. Her life just happened to be a few hundred miles away from the epicenter of his. That's all really, it was quite simple. Telling Finn goodbye, she walked out the door to the garage.

By the time Dani walked in, she had everything turned on and was grinding the coffee beans. Closing her eyes, she let the rich smell wash through her. It didn't erase the reality of her situation, but it couldn't hurt either. Grabbing the elastic off her wrist she threw her hair back in a ponytail now that it was dry. Before she had a chance to call out and ask what the special cookies were today Dani popped her head out of the kitchen and let her know.

"Pecan pie bars, and white chocolate key lime cookies today," Dani said. "How was the rest of your weekend?"

Leigha took a moment to write the cookies on the chalk board. "Ridge got a phone call and had to fly back to Nashville yesterday afternoon," she finally said.

"Damn, I'm sorry honey. How long until he comes back home?" Dani asked.

"He said a few days," Leigha answered.

"I guess he will be doing a lot of flying back and forth."

"Probably," Leigha said, but she didn't really believe it herself. "How was your Sunday?" she asked changing the subject.

"Not too bad. Silas talked all day long about Ridge and Boomer, I mean that, literally all day. I'm not even exaggerating. We had to go to the store too, he outgrew a bunch of clothes, again," Dani said shaking her head.

"Tell him to slow down, he is growing too damn fast," Leigha said with a genuine smile.

"Believe me, I've tried, it doesn't seem to work." Dani laughed before heading back into the kitchen.

Leigha breathed a sigh of relief. She just didn't feel like talking about how shitty she felt right now, not even with her best friend. By the time they opened for the day Leigha was ready for the distraction of customers. Mrs. Bowman came in like always and held court at her usual table in front of the window. Leigha kept busy straightening things and cleaning up whenever she wasn't making coffees. Tina came in just as Mrs. Bowman was leaving for the day, yelling out a goodbye to Leigha as she walked out the door.

"Have you been listening to the radio today?" Tina asked, her eyes alight with excitement.

"Nope," Leigha said shrugging.

"They're saying Ridge is back working on a new album in Nashville. When did he leave?" she asked pulling on her apron.

"He flew down yesterday," Leigha said.

"It's been like two years since he released anything new. I'm pretty excited for a new album," Tina said with a little dance.

Leigha just nodded her head. "It's been pretty slow in here today, I'm going to head back to the office for a bit. Just give me a shout if it gets too busy, alright?"

"Yeah, no problem. I got this," Tina said before turning to greet the customer walking in the door.

She left the door to her office open so she could hear if Tina needed her, even though what she really wanted to do was close it and hide away. She spent the next few hours going over the supply lists, accounts, and all the other boring responsibilities she had to deal with as a business owner. Caught up in the normal monotony of spreadsheets she could forget about Ridge for just a little while, and how much she missed him already.

When Dani stuck her head in to let her know she was leaving for the day Leigha looked at the clock in the corner of her computer screen and realized she spent longer in her office than she planned to. Standing up from her desk she followed Dani out front. Tina was wiping down the counter, and the place was completely empty of customers. They didn't close for another half hour, but Tina was getting a start on the cleaning since she clearly had the time. Leigha looked around at the gleaming machines and was quite impressed. Tina had handled it all beautifully.

"You didn't need any help?" she asked after saying goodbye to Dani.

"Nah, I've been here long enough now that I've got it all handled," Tina said with a shrug.

"I guess so. Great job today. You can go on home now, I'll finish the cleaning up," Leigha told her.

Tina smiled, and took off her apron, hanging it up on the designated hook. After she was gone Leigha looked around. This place was her dream, but it clearly could survive a day without her. Bittersweet feelings flowed through her. On one hand she felt a little useless, but on the other she was so damn proud that her baby didn't need her anymore.

By the time she flipped the open sign over to closed there wasn't much left for her to do other than shut down the cash register and take the deposit to the bank. Walking in with the pouch of money she felt like she was in her own little world. People were talking, and laughing as they shared bits of gossip, and she just didn't have it in her today to even pretend like she cared. The bank teller asked her what was wrong, and she stared at the woman for a full thirty seconds before the question filtered in.

"Oh, I've got a massive headache today." The lie tasted like bitter ashes on her tongue.

"Good thing you're heading home for the day, huh?"

This teller was newer, hadn't worked there before she left. Although Leigha saw her in here all the time, she had never bothered to learn her name. Glancing at her name tag pinned onto her shirt Leigha replied, "Basically. Thanks Ashley, have a good day." Ashley the teller smiled at her, missing that Leigha had no clue who she was until she read her name.

At home she sat on her couch and tried to distract herself by watching some television with Finn. She wasn't feeling very hungry, but since she hadn't eaten anything since the pancakes with Ridge, she made herself a grilled cheese sandwich. Finally, she couldn't take it anymore, and after rinsing her dishes and putting them in the dishwasher she walked over to where her phone sat on the counter. It was powered off, but it was still screaming silently at her all the same. Picking it up she turned it on and watched the screen start glowing. The notifications started piling up on the screen as soon as it was on. Her Mom had called again, and Ridge was persistent.

Letting her Mom worry about her wasn't something Leigha wanted to do, so she shot her

Mom a text. Letting her know that she had left her phone at home all day, to ward off another call. Her Mom replied back letting her know she was coming into the shop to see her tomorrow afternoon. Leigha told her she would see her then and sent her all her love.

She scanned through the messages from Ridge. Most of them were about the same as the ones he left yesterday. But the last few she could tell he was getting pissed.

> *Damn it, Leigha! Don't do this.*
> *You're not backing away from us.*
> *What we have isn't going away.*

She wasn't going to reply, but her thumbs were tapping out a message before she thought better of it.

> *I'm just protecting my heart Ridge.*

She hit send. His reply came back immediately. She could almost see him, phone in hand, staring at the screen fuming while he waited impatiently for her to reply.

I told you I wouldn't break it again. You don't believe me yet. But you'll see.

Leigha sat her phone back down. She didn't have anything to say to that. Ridge was still in Nashville, and he could say what he wanted, but that didn't mean it was how it was going to go. After all, he had good intentions to come back for her the first time too, but he never did.

Chapter Eighteen

Time was dragging by excruciatingly slow, and missing with Ridge had become the new normal for Leigha. After a few days he stopped trying to text or call her, and she swung back and forth between relief and annoyance. Every time her phone buzzed, she snatched it up in a silent panic that it was Ridge. She could admit that it was crazy that she wanted him to call, even though she wasn't picking the phone up when he did. She even found herself listening to his music while she laid in bed late at night. Hoping it would fill the all the spaces inside of her that Ridge being gone had left gaping wide open again. Last time she had completely avoided all his songs, going so far as to change the radio station when they came on. Now she had every single one of his albums downloaded in the library on her phone. His voice floating through the darkness in her bedroom while she curled up with Finn brought her more comfort than she would have expected. It was as if there was a tangible piece of him still there with her.

Leigha felt like she had a whole new insight

into who Ridge was now too. He wrote every single one of his songs, she knew that because she had checked online. She could hear his loneliness, and it called out to the echoing emptiness inside of her afraid that what they had was gone again. His raw anger at the mistakes he knew he was making but couldn't seem to stop himself. Ridge tapped into some of the deepest, most honest parts of himself when writing, and it stunned her as much as it helped her. A few songs she couldn't help but wonder if they were written about her. Even though it felt a tad narcissistic to assume that, but he sang a lot about melting chocolate eyes. His ex-wife had very pretty sky-blue eyes. She couldn't help but wonder what that had felt like for her, having a husband who was singing about another woman's eyes. There was no way to miss it. Of course songs weren't always about real life experiences. But sometimes they were. After all he did tell her that he would lay next to his wife at night and think of her instead.

After what felt like one of the longest weeks in recorded history Leigha couldn't stop herself and searched the gossip sights for news on what Ridge was up to down in Nashville. He was keeping a fairly low profile though, and the paparazzi had gotten tired of taking pictures of him entering or exiting his record label. It was just too mundane. He wasn't hanging out at bars, he wasn't spotted with a new love hanging onto his arm, so he just wasn't worth it to them. People wanted scandal, and excitement when they read about celebrities. There were plenty of other musicians down there living it up, and giving them juicy gossip to chase after, and exploit. At first the rumor mill was churning overtime speculating that Ridge was back in town for another chance with Suzy, but when nobody managed to catch them together the excitement died down before it had really even gotten much of a chance to start.

At work Dani had figured out that Leigha was doubting Ridge was coming back, and clearly didn't agree with her. "I'm telling you, I saw the way he looked at you, that man has got it bad. He'll be back," Dani said reassuringly.

"I thought that the last time he left here though, and look how that played out. Damn it, Dani, I don't want to always be the woman he leaves holding her heart in her hand," Leigha said with a sigh. "Loving Ridge has never been easy."

"Loving another person is never easy Leigha. Love is complicated, messy, and sometimes it guts you so deep that you don't think you'll ever be able to draw a full breath into your lungs without pain again. Ridge is not the same selfish kid with an impossible dream who left here. He is a grown man who knows exactly what he would be losing out on by letting you go this time. I know he broke your heart, hell honey, I had a front row seat to the destruction in all its terrible glory. But I also know that since he walked back into town you have been happier than I've ever seen. He had you fucking glowing from the inside out. When a man lights your soul on fire like that you'd be a damn fool to let him go," Dani said pulling another batch of deliciously fragrant sugar cookies out of the massive oven.

"I'm not just letting him go. He *left*, Dani." Leigha snatched a hot cookie off the sheet, tossing it gently back and forth on the tips of her fingers while it cooled.

"For work. He has a pretty demanding job, you know. And he has every intention of coming back, he told you that, a few times. If you're not willing to believe in him, and stick by him, then you shouldn't be with him at all. He may not be perfect, but Ridge is a good man, and not everyone is lucky enough to find one of those for their own. Stop thinking so damn much about what could go wrong, or why you think it shouldn't work. If you won't listen to your own heart, then follow his. Because I can promise you that it will lead the way home. Now get your mopey ass out of my kitchen, I've got work to do. And stop stealing my cookies before they're frosted," Dani said annoyed, and clearly dismissing her.

Leigha spent the rest of the day mulling over what Dani had said. Her friend wasn't usually so blunt about things, and she gave her some space for a while to cool off. Leigha felt selfish as hell complaining about her broken heart when Dani had her own troubles. Was she just being a coward? Breaking her own heart before Ridge even got the chance to mess everything up? That wasn't her intention, but she could admit she didn't take it very well when he told her he had to go out of town. It felt like the brick wall she had been so sure was coming all along, had popped up to surprise her, and she was running away as fast as she could to avoid colliding with it. But her feelings were moving so fast that there really was no way to pull over and avoid a crash. It was either going to work out, or she was going to be crushed. Her heart wasn't as untouchable as she thought, locked away somewhere safe from Ridge's grasp. Nope.

Even her Mom thought she was being a fool. Thinking about their conversation last night on the phone when her Mom had even suggested that if Ridge wasn't back soon Leigha should just pop down there and see what the holdup was. *Don't let him get away from you again Leigha, a love like that doesn't happen often. You've got a second chance, hold on to it with all you've got,* her Mom had said. Like it was just as easy as that. She had a business to help run, and he would think she had lost her damn mind showing up on his doorstep like that. Not that she even knew where that doorstep actually was, and she couldn't wander around town asking people either. They would definitely think she was some crazed stalker or something. Shaking her head, no she couldn't do that. Although getting her hands on him again might be worth all the trouble. Her whole body ached for that man, and she felt every single minute of the week he was gone.

Leigha was wiping up the already spotless counter with a rag for the millionth time when the kitchen door swung open. Dani walked out carrying a tray loaded down with the finished sugar cookies. They were covered in pale mint green frosting with a lovely *CS* piped in the center in navy blue.

"Those are really cute Dani. Our colors, and

our name," Leigha said, the first genuine smile in days breaking across her face, looking like the sun trying to escape out from behind the clouds.

"Thanks. They taste as good as they look too. I was thinking it might be nice to incorporate our logo more. Silas asked me last night when he was getting a Caffeinated Sprinkles shirt of his own, and it got my head going," Dani replied as she expertly stacked the scrumptious cookies in the display case. "Maybe we could put up a little stand over there with some shirts, and maybe aprons for sale."

"Yes! I really like that idea! Ooooo! Why don't we do some ceramic travel mugs too?" Leigha said getting excited about the possibilities. "And I'm sorry for being an idiot," she added leaning her head on her best friend's shoulder.

"I'm sorry for snapping at you. I'm just afraid that you're getting in the way of your own happiness, and it pisses me off because you deserve so much better," Dani said wrapping her arm around Leigha's shoulder.

"What would I do without you smacking some sense into me when I need it?" Leigha asked with a laugh.

"Oh god!" Dani said with mock horror. "I really hope we never find out," she added with a laugh. "I'm glad you like the souvenir idea."

"We could call it Caffeinated Sprinkles To-Go. Put a little sign on top of the display. Magnets might be a good one too. With our phone number on it so everyone can call orders in." Leigha added. "I'm going to run some numbers tonight, see what I can come up with."

"Excellent!" Dani said giving Leigha one last squeeze before she headed back into the kitchen.

The logo cookies were flying off the shelf all day. Everyone wanted one with their coffee, even people who normally didn't end up buying cookies. When Dani came back out of the kitchen and saw how many of them were gone Leigha suggested it might be a good idea to make them one of their regular cookie choices. Things were definitely looking up, and Leigha decided if Ridge called her again, she was going to pick the damn phone up. No more holding it in her hand staring while his name flashed across the screen. No more hiding from what was happening between them.

Chapter Nineteen

Another week passed without word from Ridge. Leigha knew that he wouldn't have stopped calling if she had answered before. She kept telling herself every morning that she would call him tonight after work, and then end up being too damn scared when the time came. Sitting on her couch, cell phone in hand she just couldn't make herself hit dial. She could rehearse the conversation in her head as many times as she wanted to, but Ridge never said or did what she thought he would. They would go off her imaginary script, and Leigha didn't know how she would be able to tell him what she needed to.

Finn was curled up in her lap, purring, while she ran her fingers through his soft orange hair. It was getting late, but she didn't have the heart to move the cat. Her thoughtful consideration didn't matter though, because as soon as the insistent knocking started on her front door he jumped off her lap and ran in the other room. Shaking her head at Finn's quick escape she turned on her porch light and peeked out the window to see who could be here

so late. The man standing on the other side of her door didn't look happy in the least. Ridge's eyes were narrowed, his jaw was clenched tight enough to have the muscle ticking, he even had his arms crossed over his chest. But Leigha didn't care one bit about the tangible waves of anger rolling off him. Fingers fumbling on the lock in her excitement it took her two tries to get it unlocked and throw open the door. Wearing her heart on her sleeve she launched herself at him. Ridge opened his arms at the last second, catching her, but quite clearly shocked at his unexpected welcome.

"OhmygodI'vemissedyousomuch," she breathed into his chest where she had her face planted.

"Wanna run that one by me again Sugar?" Ridge asked pulling them through the door and into the house.

"I said that I missed you so much," Leigha said pulling her head away and beaming up at him.

"Could've fooled me, or is ignoring phone calls how one shows someone they care these days?" he asked.

"I'm an idiot Ridge, a gigantic idiot. I realize that now, okay? I am terrified this is going to hurt, so damn bad," Leigha said staring up into his face, but not letting go of his waist.

"Leigha, I don't want to lose you again either. I'm risking that pain too. You aren't the only one in danger of a broken heart," Ridge said running his hand over her hair, roots to tips. The familiar gesture felt so right. "Being away from you was hard on me too."

"We're a long way from those kids we used to be. We had all the answers back then, and jumped in head first," Leigha said closing her eyes a moment. "But all I did trying to avoid that heart break, was cause some."

"Yeah, you did," Ridge said leaning down pressing his forehead to hers. "But I understand. We've got an awful lot of history between us, and it's not all real good. I know that."

"No, not all of it. But someone told me recently that love is never easy, its messy, and painful. But I've got a good man in my arms right now, and I think I'd like to hold onto him," Leigha whispered in a shaking voice.

"I'm still yours, Sugar. I think I've always been yours. Maybe I'm just not the kind of man who can move on," Ridge said as his lips skimmed softly across hers.

"Thank god for that," Leigha said on a sigh

and opened her mouth for his tongue to delve inside.

The kiss started out soft and sweet, but their ever-increasing hunger for each other had it morphing into deeply passionate quickly. Her hands gripped the back of his head holding on while he took everything she gave him. Leigha's blood felt like molten lava pumping through her veins. Ridge tipped her head back even further, changing the angle as he devoured her. Shivers went cascading down her spine, anticipating all the pleasure his kiss promised. Ridge reached behind his head and pulled his shirt quickly off, his lips crashing back down to hers. The desperate longing for each other was filled with so much heat. The rest of their clothes came off in a flurry of urgency, landing in discarded heaps all over Leigha's living room.

His mouth left hers to trail hotly down her neck, and she tipped her head to give him better access to her sensitive skin. "Do you want me Sugar?" he asked.

"Yes," she moaned.

"How much?" he asked as his teeth skimmed up her neck to nibble on her ear lobe.

"So fucking much," Leigha said.

"Is your pussy already wet for me?" Ridge asked.

Leigha nodded her head, loving it when he talked dirty to her.

"Show me," Ridge whispered into her ear, his breath tickling it and making her shiver again. He pulled back enough to meet her eyes.

Seeing his desire for her burning in the green depths she grabbed his hand. She ran his hand down the front of her body, and between her legs. He kept his hand completely still, and she slid it between her folds, drenching his fingers. His eyebrow flicked up, but he still didn't move his hand. Leigha circled her hips, grinding her clit down into his palm while the tips of his fingers hovered at her entrance.

"Are you gonna fuck my hand Sugar?" Ridge growled out.

All Leigha could do was nod her head. Drowning in his eyes, her body on fire. Ridge curled two of his fingers up sending them inside of her pussy hitting her G-spot perfectly right. Leigha gasped and moved her hips faster, her hand gripping his wrist, holding him where she needed him most. Her legs started shaking as the pressure deep inside grew. She was panting, hurrying to drag air into her lungs, as her body raced towards the promise building within. Leigha cried out as the orgasm washed over her in near violent pulses. Her knees gave out, but Ridge picked her up before she could face plant into the carpet of her living room floor. His dick pressed hotly between them, and Leigha needed to feel the thick length of him in her with a near painful ache.

"Need you Ridge. Need you right fucking now," she said urgently.

Ridge nodded his head and lowered her body until he slipped through her wetness. Using his hands on her hips he lifted her up and down impaling her with his dick, which had the added benefit of her clit rubbing against him with each stroke. Leigha dug her heels into his ass, and her head fell forward onto his shoulder as she struggled to absorb everything she was feeling. Her pleasure receptors were definitely working overtime tonight. Her fingers were digging into his scalp, but she couldn't make herself let go. Nothing in her whole life had felt as big as what was building between them. Ridge was panting with each powerful stroke.

Her screams bounced around the room, echoing off the walls. Leigha was sure the neighbors could hear, and she didn't give a damn. Being with Ridge was primal, it woke up everything inside of her, and made her feel so good it bordered on pain. Her body started trembling, as she got closer and closer to the climax.

"It's time to come Sugar," Ridge growled in her ear. "I wanna feel your pussy squeezing me."

His dirty words nudged her over the precipice she had been balanced on, sending her slamming headfirst into the biggest orgasm of her life, so far. Her inner muscles milked him as her body was filled with wave after tingling wave of pleasure. Ridge squeezed her ass, pulling the cheeks apart as he worked her even faster over his dick. He let out a hoarse cry and she felt the warmth of his orgasm filling her.

Everything felt intensified, like she was drunk on the way he made her feel as she struggled to breathe evenly. Ridge took a few shaky steps forward, and sat abruptly down, Leigha straddling him, still locked intimately together. He tucked her wild hair behind her ear and gave the ends a gentle tug. "I love you Leigha, so fucking much it's like I can't breathe sometimes," he whispered.

She looked down into his beautiful green eyes, and let the words settle over her like water rushing over her parched soul, soothing all the cracks. Leigha nodded her head, and tears filled her eyes. She opened her mouth to respond, but Ridge held his hand up, fingers pressing against her lips.

"You don't have to say anything, not right now. I just needed to say it, needed you to know it. If you say it right now then it will just be like you echoing it back to me. I want it to feel like its ripping up from your soul, and there is no way you could keep it in a minute longer when you finally say it."

Chapter Twenty

Leigha slept peacefully, curled into Ridge's warm body in her bed. Being locked within the comfort of his arms settled all the frayed edges inside of her soul. There was no room for fear or worries to invade the space. It was just the two of them, the love he professed to her, and the promise for so much more still between them. She reached for him again in the middle of the night, with the need burning hotly through her veins. He answered her, his demands always mirroring her own desires. Now that she wasn't working so hard all the time to keep the walls up around her heart she could admit to herself that being with him breathed life back into her. She had been so afraid of anchoring him down, like dead weight in his life, tying him somewhere he shouldn't be. Afraid also of the dragging weight of heartbreak on her soul she thought was inevitably coming her way. Instead she felt like she was floating, flying recklessly, and gloriously through the sky. Being with Ridge was right, had always been right for Leigha. She was finally understanding that. Maybe he always was the right guy, all along, the timing just wasn't ever right before.

The alarm started buzzing early in the morning, demanding attention. Half asleep Leigha swung her arm out in a practiced move with perfect aim, shutting it off. Stretching as she sat up, she looked down at where Ridge was still asleep next to her. His brown hair was disheveled from sleep, and her hands cruising through it the last time he was moving inside of her. He hadn't shaved his face in a few days, at least, if the stubble along his jaw was any indication. She wondered if he was too busy to bother, or if he had forgotten about it entirely. With a smile tugging on her face Leigha, remembered the first time Ridge attempted to grow a beard. Like most teenage guys he started shaving as soon as there was peach fuzz sprouting up on his face, trying desperately to encourage more growth. He got it in his head over the winter their junior year that a beard would keep his face warmer in the blustery Michigan weather, and make him look like a bad ass, of course. After a whole month without a razor touching his face he had what looked like three scraggly hairs on his upper lip, a half dozen on his chin, and another three or four scattered on each of his cheeks. To say it was less than a success was an understatement. Running her hand across his square jaw, feeling the hairs prickle deliciously against her fingertips she got out of bed. It finally grew in nice, and he did look beyond sexy with it.

Glancing at the clock and a quick calculation on time Leigha gave a little sigh and walked out of the bedroom to grab a shower. She would have preferred some company truth be told, but if she invited him to join her it would take much longer, and she would be late. As much as she wouldn't mind some steamy shower sex with Ridge to start her day she had a coffee shop to open. People were counting on her. Once she had finished her routine of washing her hair and body she turned the water off, and pulled the curtain back to reach for a towel. Ridge stood there leaning against the bathroom counter, her towel already in his hand. She took it from him and wrapped it around her body, tucking the end in to hold it up. He had pulled on his boxer shorts from last night, but nothing else. The sight didn't exactly help her reign in the libido that had just been clamoring for shower sex.

"You didn't wake me up," he said. His voice was still rumbling and deep from sleep. Just the sound of it made her clench her thighs together in anticipation.

"I figured you could grab an extra few

minutes while I showered," Leigha said, grabbing a second towel and wrapping her hair up in it.

"Thanks, but I'd rather have spent those extra minutes in the shower with you," he said leaning down to press a soft kiss to the top of her shoulder.

"I'll set my alarm for a little earlier next time," Leigha said with a smile. "I've got an extra toothbrush you can use." She opened a drawer and grabbed the unopened box out handing it to him. "I always keep a spare, ever since I came home from work and found Finn dragging mine through the house one day."

Ridge was laughing as he took the toothbrush out of her hand and opened the box. "Yeah, I can see that being necessary after a sight like that."

They brushed their teeth at her sink in a comfortable silence. Their eyes kept meeting each other's in the mirror. "Are you hungry?" she asked as she set the toothbrush back in its holder.

"How about I scramble up some eggs real quick while you get dressed and ready for work?" Ridge replied.

"Sure," she said smiling. He leaned down and kissed her smiling mouth quickly before walking out of the bathroom. Leigha stood there a moment feeling the shimmering flutter inside of a dozen butterflies taking flight. "Yep. I'm in deep," she whispered to her reflection.

Back in her bedroom Leigha checked the weather on her cell phone. It had been warm so far as they headed into spring, but with Michigan you never really knew. Deciding on the lightweight short sleeved sweater in a sunny yellow with a pair of dark jeans. Looking in the mirror she decided the color matched how she felt inside. Bright, happy, and filled with warmth. Walking back into the bathroom she tipped her head upside down, releasing her dark hair from the towel and gave it a quick shake. She ran a wide tooth comb through it, before slathering moisturizer on her face. Grabbing an elastic from the same drawer she had pulled a toothbrush out for Ridge, she shoved it on her wrist for later.

The smell of bacon had her smiling as she walked into the kitchen. "Thought you said eggs?"

"Got those too. But you had the bacon, so I figured what the hell," he said with a shrug. Ridge's back was to her, as he turned the eggs over with a spatula in the pan. The bacon was popping in a second pan in front of him. He glanced over his shoulder at her and the look in his eyes nearly stopped her heart. There was wonder in those beautiful green depths. Seeing a man look at you with his eyes full of heat was thrilling, exhilarating to be sure. But watching awe bloom in his gaze as he took you in wasn't something to be missed, and the slow smile that spread across his face was worth more than all the money in the bank. "Damn, you're absolutely stunning Leigha. I am one lucky man."

Going on impulse Leigha walked over to him as he turned back to the stove, and wrapped her arms around his middle, pressing a kiss right between his shoulder blades. "You're not so bad yourself Ridge Bradley."

"Glad you think so," he said as he reached over to grab plates from the cupboard.

They ate the simple breakfast standing up in the kitchen. Leigha loaded the dishwasher while Ridge went to get dressed. He invited her over for dinner at his house that night as they walked out of the house together. She, for Caffeinated Sprinkles, and Ridge headed out of town for home. On the quick drive Leigha cranked the radio and sang along, off key, but loudly to the music. Her soul was drenched in light, and she was basking happily in the rays.

When Dani walked in the door a little while later, her arms loaded down with boxes of goodies she stopped and watched Leigha smiling dreamily as she ground the coffee beans for the day. Sighing happily, she walked in, she kissed her best friend on the cheek before heading back into the kitchen. "Ridge," she whispered as she set the boxes down on the worktable. Turning on the kitchen radio, she smiled. "Spring is in the air, and it's gonna be a damn good day."

Chapter Twenty-One

L eigha picked up the phone with a smile in her voice. "Good afternoon, Caffeinated Sprinkles, how may we help you?"

"Hey honey," came the voice on the other line.

"Hi Mom. What's up? Is everything okay?" she asked, wondering why her Mom wasn't calling her cell phone like she usually did.

"Of course, everything is fine honey. Your Dad and I just want to see you, come on over for dinner tonight." Leigha noticed she wasn't being asked, so much as being told what to do.

"Tonight? I uh, kind of already have plans," Leigha said remembering Ridge had invited her over for the evening.

"I heard Ridge was back in town again, bring him along with you. Then you can do the rest of those plans later on in the evening," her Mom said with a knowing laugh. Leigha had hoped to avoid this situation longer, maybe even forever if she could manage it.

"I love how casually you talk about my sex life, Mom," Leigha said with more than a little embarrassment. "But it doesn't sound like I have much of a choice," she said feeling her mood droop.

"You're not a child anymore Leigha, of course you have a choice. If you don't want to come home for dinner with your parents, then we can bring dinner to you. Will you be at your house, or his? And everyone should have a satisfying sex life honey, it's one of the best parts of being alive." Her Mom easily maneuvered her into a corner.

"Wow, quite nicely done Mom. I hope I'm half as smooth when I have children," Leigha said with a sigh, and ignoring the other comment. She was happy her parents had a strong marriage, but she didn't really need to know about what went on in their bedroom.

"Oh, years of practice honey, years of practice. So see you at seven then?" her Mom said with a completely guiltless laugh.

"Yeah, do you need me to bring anything? Desert, wine, copious amounts of hard liquor?" she said thinking getting sloshed might not be a bad idea.

"I've got it completely covered, I'm making a cobbler, a la mode too. Stop being so dramatic silly girl. It will be just fine. We just want to see how Ridge has been all these years, catch up."

Translation, grill him mercilessly. Hopefully they made it all the way through dinner to desert, her Mom did make the absolute best peach cobbler around, so that was something at least.

Leigha hung up with her Mom as some customers walked in the door making it ding musically. She plastered a smile on her face as she greeted them, even though the conversation with her Mom had tarnished the lovely shine of her mood today. After getting the coffees, lattes, and pretty cookies for everyone in line she picked up her cell phone.

Mom called to let me know they're expecting us for dinner at their house tonight.

Leigha didn't have to wait long for Ridge to reply to her text.

OK. Dinner at your folks house it is then.

Leigha stared at her phone shaking her head, maybe Ridge wasn't fully understanding the situation. But he surprised her with a second text.

They just want to scope me out, see what my intentions with you are. So I've got nothing to worry about.

Nothing to worry about?

Nope. ;) Meet you at your place and we can drive over there together, present a united front. Later, Sugar.

Everyone had gone completely crazy, Leigha thought to herself. Sighing, she let it go. There wasn't a damn thing she could do about it right now, in the middle of the day at work. Today was Tina's day off, so when Dani left for the day to pick up Silas from the sitter's house, she was glad to be all alone. The routine of cleaning helped settle some of her anxiety about dinner. It was comforting to let her mind go wandering wherever it wanted while she swept and mopped the day's layer of grime off the floors. By the time she finished with everything and was walking out to take the deposit to the bank she felt better about the daunting prospect ahead. But only marginally.

At home she had time to make sure Finn had his dinner, and some cuddles before she heard Ridge's truck pull in. When he rapped his knuckles against the door Leigha called out for him to come on in. Ridge looked especially good tonight, he'd put on a deep mossy green button-down shirt, and a dark pair of blue jeans. The boots where still the same though, and it made everything knotted up inside Leigha loosen. He watched her perusal of him with a crooked smirk, and a smile shining in his eyes.

"Ready to go Sugar?"

"Yeah, we probably should," Leigha said sounding resigned to her fate.

"Oh, come on. They liked me before. This is hardly the firing squad we are about to face," Ridge said pulling her to his body with a hand at the back of her neck and pressing a sweet kiss to her temple.

"I know, I know. I'm just, well, shit, I don't know why I'm so nervous about it. It's not like I need permission to be with you," Leigha said as she reached up and smoothed her hand over his hair.

"But you want their approval. It's alright, baby, I understand, really," Ridge said. "But even if we don't have it, I'm all the way in this Leigha. I meant it when I said I loved you. I'm a lot of things, but a player has never been one of them."

The steely determination written all over his face told her he meant every word of what he said. Nodding her head, she went up on her tippy toes, and reaching up she pressed her lips softly against his. "Then let's get this the hell over with."

Neither of them said much on the drive over to her parents' house. Sitting next to Ridge in a pickup truck brought back so many memories. This one had bucket seats with a wide center console between them, instead of a bench seat so she couldn't sit pressed against his side like she used to when they were teenagers. As he pulled into the driveway of her childhood home, she remembered coming home later than curfew after the homecoming dance. She was more nervous now than she was then strangely enough. Back then every extra minute spent with Ridge was worth any cost. Now, she understood that if this didn't go well it would cost her something she wasn't ready to lose. Ridge put the truck into park and hopped quickly out. She watched him jog briskly around the hood to come over to her side and open her door. When she climbed down, he closed the door, gave the ends of her hair a quick tug, for encouragement and wrapped his arm around her waist. Facing the house Leigha felt Ridge take a deep breath to steady himself. That little bit of nervousness in him helped smooth out some of the sharp edges of her own.

Her Dad was the first to step out onto the front porch as they made their way up the steps. "There's my girl," he said with a smile on his face, all but beaming at Leigha. Without any hesitation she stepped up into his arms and he gave her a squeeze. Her Mom opened the door as her Dad was releasing her. "It's been too long darling, you need to come by more often," he chided. That was nothing new, he never thought she visited enough, and Leigha knew that her Dad would always miss seeing her every day.

"It's about time you came by to see me Ridge Bradley," her Mom said walking over and giving him a pat on the cheek.

Ridge smiled and handed her the tissue wrapped bouquet of colorful spring blooms that was already sitting on the console when Leigha got in earlier. "My apologies Sherri, I should have come out to see you sooner."

"Sure should have," she said with a nod. "Thank you, Ridge. Such pretty flowers, look Rob, aren't these lovely?" she asked turning towards her husband.

He nodded his head slightly. Rob Taylor was still a rather fit man, even well into his fifties. His once dark blonde hair was mostly gray now, but his deep-set hazel eyes missed nothing. The lines etched into his face only served to make him look distinguished, showing the map of a life well lived. He was a dependable man, gentle and caring. That didn't mean there wasn't a stubborn streak in him a mile wide, that he had passed down to his only daughter. And everyone knew he would do anything in this world for 'his girls' as he called them. "A word Ridge?"

The two men looked at each other for a few beats while Leigha held her breath. Ridge looked down at Leigha, meeting her eyes and said, "I'll be along inside in a few minutes." Leigha may not have completely understood all the male dynamics at play here, since she lacked the required equipment dangling between her legs for that, but she was smart enough to know they needed to work it out themselves.

Laying a hand on his chest, over the top of his heart she nodded her head. "Need any help in the kitchen Mom?" Leigha asked turning towards her Mom. Sherri nodded her head and gave Rob's arm a squeeze before opening the door back up. Holding it open for Leigha the two women walked inside, leaving the men their privacy.

Leigha circled the dining room table setting their plates down. It was a stunning long oval of polished mahogany that seated eight around it comfortably. She knew it had been a wedding present from her late grandparents to her parents many years ago. It was still a beautiful table, and she ran her fingertips over the shiny top of it wondering, "Mom, did your parents always like Dad?"

Carrying over the meatloaf her Mom let out a startled laugh. "Good lord, no honey. My Dad thought he drove his car too fast, and that he would never be good enough for me. My Mom didn't understand why he wore his hair so long and shaggy, thought it meant he was selling drugs."

"Dad? A drug dealer?" Leigha laughed at the image of her solid, pillar of the community father hawking drugs on a street corner. "But they came around."

"Eventually, yes. They could see how much he loved me, it was pretty hard to miss, and that was all they really wanted. Was for me to be happy. Are you worried about what they're saying out there?" she asked.

"Absolutely, Mom," Leigha answered immediately.

"Honey, we want the same things for you my parents wanted for me. Happiness, and a man to treat you the way you deserve. We always liked Ridge, you know that, but the truth of it is he did break your heart once upon a time. Your Dad especially is really struggling with that. Knowing that man out there could crush his little girl's heart again scares the living hell out of him," her Mom answered walking back into the kitchen for the rest of the food.

Leigha followed her Mom, grabbing the gravy boat, and bowl of green beans since her Mom already had the mashed potatoes in her hands. "What about you?"

"I know Ridge didn't go into it back then to hurt you on purpose. He was a little careless maybe, but he was young and so blinded by his dreams. I guess I can understand that the path your lives took was a winding one, and hope that maybe it's finally brought you to where you're supposed to be," she said wisely, putting her hands on her hips. "That doesn't mean I won't help your Dad bury his body out back if need be," she said without blinking, patted Leigha on the cheek and walked back into the kitchen.

Leigha was still staring after her Mom, feeling a little bit dumbstruck when the front door opened. Her Dad walked in and brushed a kiss to her forehead as he passed by heading into the kitchen. Ridge stopped behind her and wrapped his arms around her body. Leaning in he whispered, "All good Sugar, you can relax now."

"My Mom just told me she would help my Dad bury your body in the backyard if he had to kill you," Leigha said in a mumble leaning back into his comforting warmth. She loved the way his larger body all but surrounded her.

Ridge let out a rich full-throated laugh that rumbled through his chest that was still pressed against her back. "Guess it's a damn good thing he decided homicide wasn't on tap for tonight then."

Chapter Twenty-Two

Laying in Ridge's bed hours later, tucked under the covers with his arm slung across her waist, his body curving into her back, Leigha couldn't manage to find sleep. Her body was delightfully exhausted, Ridge was full of stamina, and always completely rocked her world. But her mind was still floating, stubbornly refusing to drift off to sleep. She could tell from the deep, even puffs of breath stirring her hair that Ridge was fast asleep behind her. She could always go down and make herself some tea, but that meant leaving the warmth of the bed. Leigha found she really didn't want to leave the bed. So she stared out the window at the moon and stars wrapped in Ridge's arms instead.

There was a time, not that long ago, that she wondered if she would ever have this. A man wrapped around her, with her body still humming happily from the things he had done to it. There is so much magic in this feeling, the totally blissed-out aftermath of good orgasms. The kind you don't have to give yourself. Every single inch of her skin was practically glowing. Sex with Ridge was so far past phenomenal Leigha wasn't sure there was even a word for it, and if so she definitely didn't know it. He was a demanding and dominant lover, but never selfish, and that suited her needs just fine. She could trust that wherever he was taking her sexually she was up for the ride. Some men played at dominance like a game, thinking they were alpha enough. But it was all just posturing, and pretend chest beating. Ridge was different. He had a very specific taste sexually, and nothing had ever made her feel more completely, beautifully feminine than when he took her like that. He worshiped her body, every single time.

Looking back on their sex before she wasn't surprised. They might have been just teenagers, riding high on hormones in the bed of his pickup truck, fumbling through. But it was never like what she heard from her friends at school. They all talked about their first time as being disappointing, just something to check off the 'to do' list of growing up. It wasn't like that between them, even that very first time. Not that every single moment felt amazing. Leigha had expected it to really hurt, considering the size of his dick. There had been a moment of so much pressure it made her gasp, and tears gather in her eyes, but that had faded quickly. Ridge had gone slow and easy with the actual sex, but he spent so much time playing with her, and pleasing her beforehand that she was all but mush when he finally took her virginity. Even being a virgin himself, he managed to keep it together long enough to make it good for her. A true rarity, even among full grown adult men. Ridge was a man who liked taking control, and once he had it, thankfully, he always knew what to do with it. But it was really that control was just him taking care of her.

She could admit thinking about it now that he ruined her for other men, even way back then. The few times she had let another man touch her in the years that came between then and now, it always left her acutely disappointed. Her body always craved this man tucked around her right now, always. Even when her bruised heart wanted nothing to do with him ever again. Smiling in the dark she breathed the scent of him deep into her lungs. Well, her heart wasn't very strong in that resolve anymore, and Leigha was finding that was fine by her. Fighting something that felt this damn right all the way down into her bones was a waste of time. They deserved this happiness, damn it. She deserved it.

Ridge mumbled something softly and pulled her body even closer to his. She thought he was just talking in his sleep at first. Until his hand came up to cup and mold her breast. "How come you're not sleeping baby?"

"My mind was happy to wander around instead," she replied as he turned her over until they were face to face.

"Guess I didn't wear you out enough. Where did your mind go?" he asked brushing the hair gently away from her face. In the moonlight his eyes were the deep green of shadows along the forest floor, and Leigha fell happily into their endless depths.

"Us. Our first time. I was looking up at the moon and remembering. I never told you how lucky I felt because all of the girls talked about just getting it over with. That the first time is never any good. It was always going to be special between us, but it was good too. You made sure of that," Leigha said running her hand over his chest. She loved feeling the tingle in her palm from sliding across the hair growing there.

His hand resting on her hip pulled her even closer to him. "Well, I wanted to show you how fucking lucky I knew I was to be inside of you, and if I didn't make it worth it then you might not let me back in again. Remember that moment before I started to actually move?"

"Yeah, you leaned down and rested your forehead against mine. I thought you were giving me a minute to adjust to how full you felt all the way inside of me," Leigha said leaning in and pressing a kiss over his heart. His laugh rumbled out, surprising her, and she looked up at him.

"Not quite. I actually forgot how to breathe because every damn nerve in my body was screaming. I could've ended it right then, it felt so damn good. I wasn't prepared for it to be like that, I mean like every other guy I jacked off all the time. So I figured I knew. I had no fucking clue. It was so much better than anything I'd ever felt, or even imagined, and I imagined being inside of you a lot. But then I looked down at your beautiful brown eyes, shining with so much trust, giving me this precious gift, and knew I needed to make you feel exactly as good as I did," Ridge said tipping her face up, his fingers threading into her hair at the back of her neck.

"I didn't know that," Leigha said feeling moved by his words, and turned on by their proximity. Her tongue peaked out to lick across her bottom lip. She could feel his dick pressing into her stomach, the hard length of it blazing hot against her skin.

"It meant as much to me as it did to you," Ridge whispered as he scraped his lips back and forth across hers exactly where her tongue had just been.

Leigha lifted her leg and wrapped it around his hip, pulling him even closer. She tried to angle her hip so he could slide inside. It had only been a little while, but her pussy already felt like it was aching with need. Ridge stilled her hips with his hand, keeping her in place as he finally kissed her. There was need, and hunger in the kiss, but Leigha knew he was giving her more. She felt everything he was pouring into her, all the love he felt, without any words. There were so many butterflies in her stomach now it was a wonder they didn't manage to break free and fly off into the night eager to dance in the moon beams. When her need for Ridge was so intense it neared pain, he shifted his hips. Leigha gasped into his mouth as she felt the thick head of his dick slide through her drenched folds. She waited for him to slip inside, but he didn't do that. Rolling his hips against hers Ridge teased her swollen clit instead.

Fingers grasping his shoulders, needing that connection, Leigha watched his eyes. Her heart beating rapidly, she moaned his name. "Ridge."

"Right here Sugar. I ever tell you how much I love your little clit? It's always so damn receptive to everything I do," Ridge said with a sexy smirk.

Leigha couldn't say anything, her brain had stepped out for a break, and she simply had no words left. He leaned down to lick her bottom lip and draw it into his mouth, his eyes never leaving hers. She shuddered, her whole body alive with sensations singing through her. Leigha's hips were trying to buck greedily towards Ridge as she chased the orgasm building deep inside of her.

"I got you Sugar," Ridge said his grip tightening on her hip, not letting her move.

"More!" Leigha cried out. "I need more!"

Ridge didn't say anything, he just scraped his teeth along the side of her neck, as his dick kept sliding tortuously slow against her clit. The tension building inside of her, tighter and tighter. Her breath was coming quickly now, in desperate gasps. Finally, it crested, the lines tying her together snapped, and all the tension swirling around inside of her flew out in great pulsing quakes as she came with a scream.

Before she could come down from the dizzying heights the orgasm dragged her up to Ridge was inside of her with a quick push of his hips. Her nails digging into his skin now, she held on as he moved deep and fast. It was such a departure from the slow glide against her earlier that she couldn't keep up. Leigha was lost to the sensations pummeling her senses, closing her eyes she came a second time, this orgasm even more intense than the first one.

This time it was Ridge calling out. "More," he growled as he pulled out of her. Leigha didn't even have time to register the loss before he flipped her over onto her stomach, pulled her wrists above her head and slammed back into her. He held both of her wrists easily in one large hand, the other one pressing the small of her back down. He pumped in and out faster and faster, his breath coming in noisy pants above her. With this new position, her body flat on the bed, ass angled up to meet his thrusts, he hit her G-spot with every single demanding stroke. It was all Leigha could do to drag air in and out of her burning lungs.

"You're so fucking wet, Sugar. Tell me how much you like this," Ridge growled.

"Don't stop," Leigha managed to moan out. "So good, you feel so good Ridge."

Ridge smacked her ass with the hand that was holding her down. The quick sting only added to the layers of sensations. "Shit," Leigha gasped as her whole body started shaking.

"You gonna come for me again?" Ridge asked as he pounded into her.

Leigha nodded her head, her muscles straining for release.

"Words, baby, give me the words," Ridge grunted.

"Yes!" Leigha screamed arching her back as the orgasm ripped through her. Her whole world narrowed down to the feeling of Ridge moving inside of her, and the consuming pleasure he gave her. The orgasm stretched endlessly on, until she wasn't sure if it was one, or if she was coming over and over again. Lost deep inside of herself she thought she heard Ridge shout, before he filled her with heat, his body pressing hers even further into the bed.

Ridge released her wrists, leaning down over her and pressing a kiss against the nape of her neck. Pulling out of her he rolled them over. Laying on his back he pulled Leigha into his side, wrapping an arm around her.

Leigha couldn't form words if she tried. She smiled up at him as the multiple orgasms finally dragged her into a deeply exhausted, satisfied sleep.

"You'll sleep better now Sugar," Ridge

whispered as her eyes closed.

Chapter Twenty-Three

Ridge dropped Leigha off at home early the next morning, after an amazingly energetic shower together, so she didn't have to wear the same clothes to work two days in a row. He mentioned something about getting back to meet a contractor out at his house as he told her goodbye. Leigha spent some time petting and cuddling Finn as she got dressed for the day. She felt a little guilty about spending so much time away from him, but he didn't seem to be holding it against her. Thinking it might be a good idea to have Ridge over at her place tonight she braided her hair in a long tail down her back. Her back yard might not be very large, being right in town, but it was fenced so Boomer could come along, and they didn't need to worry about him getting away.

She was smiling thinking about her plans for tonight when she slowly backed her car out of the garage. Looking over she saw Ty in his driveway looking like he was about to get in his truck. He gave her a quick wave and a careful smile. She could see he was uncomfortable. Seeing that had her feeling a little bad about the way they left things last time, and not wanting to lose a friend, she hit the button sending her window gliding down.

"Hey Ty, hows it going?" she called out.

He walked over to her car, his smile a little less tight around the edges now. "Mornin' Leigha. The weather looks like it's finally turned. I think we're done with the damn snow for the season."

"Me too. Haven't seen you in Caffeinated Sprinkles in a bit. Did ya give up drinking coffee?" she asked him, knowing he wasn't coming in because he was avoiding her.

"Not exactly. I've uh, been getting it from the gas station," he admitted, ducking his head sheepishly. "Figured it was for the best."

"Ty. We'll never be a couple, which I'm thinking you get loud and clear now. But we've always been friends. That coffee is shit, and we both know it." He nodded at her and they shared a laugh. "So I'll be seeing you for your caffeine fix then?"

"Yeah, I'll be in, probably after seeing what Ridge wants done to his new place," he said easily.

Leigha should have put it together sooner. "He mentioned having someone come by the house. I didn't realize it was you though."

"Yeah, he didn't really tell me what he wanted

done when he called yesterday," Ty said with a shrug. "Well, I'd better let you get going. Can't be late opening up the place," he said with a friendly wink and walked back over to his truck.

Leigha pulled out of her driveway with a final wave and drove the few blocks across town. She was wondering what Ridge was having done to his house, but feeling happy about it because that was another reason to hope he was staying in town. People didn't just fix up a house and move usually. Well, flippers do, but Ridge wasn't one of those, it wasn't like he needed the money. Besides, his house was already really nice, it would sell just fine so there was no need. Which meant logically, that he was changing something to make it more his, to fit his needs.

By the time Dani walked in a little bit later, her arms loaded down with today's tasty confections Leigha was wearing a perma-grin. "Look at you, I take it dinner at your parent's house went good?" Dani asked as she maneuvered through to the kitchen.

Leigha knew from experience not to offer to help her friend carry the boxes in. Dani didn't appreciate it, in fact it usually pissed her off when someone thought maybe she couldn't handle it. "It did. There was some tension when we first got there, but Dad had a man to man chat outside." Leigha used air quotes with her fingers around man to man with a cheeky grin. "And when they came back in, I guess they worked it all out. Which I was pretty damn happy about since my Mom told me she would've helped Dad bury Ridge's body out back if they didn't." Leigha said laughing. "Because I kind of like his body."

"She didn't!" Dani exclaimed, just as shocked as Leigha herself had been. "And we can all see how much you like his body by the just fucked smile on your face all the time." She winked at Leigha.

"Oh, she absolutely did," Leigha said.

"Damn. Momma Sherri is definitely a ride or die chick," Dani said and they both spent a few moments laughing.

"I guess that's how you have a happy marriage for so long. Knowing where all the bodies are," Leigha said.

"Yeah, because she helped bury them!" Dani said, and they laughed all over again.

"So, what totally delicious goodies are hiding in these boxes?" Leigha asked as Dani started opening them.

"Strawberry coffee cake crumble top muffins, and some to die for chocolate truffle cookies," Dani said.

Leigha looked inside the boxes at all the pretty cookies and muffins inside, making sure to take a great big whiff. "Damn, those look fabulous. Dani girl, you are a genius," she said slinging her arm affectionately around her friend. "Once Tina gets in, I'm going to hide back in the office and get to work making our souvenir station a reality."

"I've got a good feeling about it. It's gonna be a hit, I just know it," Dani said leaning her head on Leigha's shoulder. "Tell me, how do you look more rested than I do, when I know you were up half of the night screaming out Ridge's name?"

Leigha laughed. "Great sex is good for the soul, and the complexion too I guess." She released Dani and she started loading up the trays for the display case out front.

"I guess so. I'll leave all that to you though. Too much hassle. I'll stick with my vibrator for now," Dani said.

"Someone is going to come along and change your mind about that. It would be a real shame if you never fell in love again," Leigha said with all seriousness. "You're such a great catch after all," she added with a wink lightening the mood.

"Damn right I am," Dani said before shooing

Leigha out of the kitchen.

Leigha was back in her office completely caught up in cost comparisons on suppliers for personalized travel coffee mugs. She figured the knock on her door was either Dani or Tina, and called out without even turning around towards the door, "Yeah?"

"Damn Sugar, you look hot as hell. I know you own this place and all, but seeing you like this, looking all in-fucking-charge does things to me," Ridge said leaning against the door. There was a sexy smirk on his face, and it had goosebumps leaping out all over her skin. "Think I could convince you to let me bend you over that desk?"

"Not on your life. The health department would have my ass on a platter for that," Leigha said with a giant grin. "I wouldn't say no to a kiss though."

Ridge walked over to her with a knowing strut. "You'd like it though," he said before pulling her up out of the chair and leaning into her.

She'd offered a kiss, and he gave her that, and then some. Ridge all but ravished her with just his lips and tongue, leaving no corner of her mouth untouched. By the time he pulled away she was wondering if she could orgasm from just that kiss alone. "I most definitely would," she said feeling more than a little breathless.

"Ty said he saw you this morning when he was out at my house," he said, just barely above a whisper, still holding her close.

Leigha just stared at Ridge for a moment, letting her lust-drunk brain sober up. "Yeah, he ah, he was leaving at the same time I was. We chatted for a couple of minutes, it was only a little bit awkward." He leaned in and pressed soft, barely there kisses down her neck. "What is he gonna do for you?" she mumbled out around a moan.

Ridge chuckled at her response. "I'm putting in a recording studio."

Leigha pulled all the way away from Ridge. "A what?"

"A small recording studio, in the basement. It's all fully finished down there already, so it won't be as much work."

"Why?" Leigha asked and held her breath. She really needed to hear him say the words out loud again.

"Because I'm staying. I've told you that," he said tracing a finger across her jaw. "I know you didn't believe me, but I meant it."

Leigha's eyes shimmered with tears for a

second, she blinked to hold them off. "I believe you now," she whispered feeling more of the wall surrounding her heart crack and crumble away.

"About damn time!" he said yanking her back to him in a hug, and swinging her around in a joyful circle.

"So I was thinking you should spend the night at my house tonight? You can bring Boomer along too. My yard is fenced, he can play out there. Not that I expect you to lock him out there the whole time, he can come inside. Maybe bring along some toys, and a bone or something too. That way he would be comfortable," Leigha said rambling.

Ridge smiled and kissed her again. "Alright, Boomer and I will come over to your place. I'm in the mood for tacos, how about I pick up the stuff, and we make some for dinner?"

Leigha nodded her head, her lips still buzzing from the last kiss. "Okay."

"Good. See you later Sugar," he said before walking out.

Leigha stepped out of her office to watch him go. He turned at the front door and gave her a wave, with a cocky eyebrow lift saying he knew she would be watching the way he walked out into the mid-afternoon sunshine. Next to her Tina sighed, the sound full of female appreciation.

"That is some man," she said longingly.

"He really is. Oh, and Tina, he's all mine too," Leigha said with a smile.

"Yeah, you're lucky as hell too," Tina said laughing. "Wouldn't mind finding me a man like that someday."

"Believe me, I know it. Give it time girl, your man will come along," Leigha said as she walked back to her office to try and get more work done. It would be a struggle though with the way Ridge had fried every one of her brain cells.

At home Leigha was having a pep talk with Finn. Trying to prepare him for his introduction to Boomer. She was a little nervous they wouldn't get along. She heard Ridge's truck pull in the drive, and took a deep breath. "Here goes nothing," she told Finn as she walked to the front door.

Ridge had Boomer on a leash, and he was sitting politely on her doorstep. Leigha leaned down to pet him as Finn jumped off the couch to walk over and investigate. Boomer gave a happy little whine, his tail thumping against the step with gusto betraying his excitement. "Come on in," Leigha said.

Ridge and Boomer stepped inside, and he shut the door behind them. They both watched as their pets sniffed each other. Boomer was clearly happy to make friends. When Finn rubbed himself along Boomer's side as he circled the dog Leigha gave a sigh of relief. She looked up, and Ridge was staring at her with the goofiest grin on his face. It reminded her of when he was much younger, the happiness shining through him was so clear and almost innocent.

"They're making friends," he said. Her heart lurched a little more inside of her chest. Ridge unhooked the leash from Boomer's collar leaving him free to play with Finn.

Leigha walked over to him and wrapped her arms around his waist, laying her head on Ridge's chest. She could hear his heart beating against her ear, strong and steady. His arms came around her without hesitation. "So, tacos?" she said looking up into his face.

"Yeah, tacos," Ridge said. "As soon as I run back out to the truck and grab the bag. Didn't want my arms full in case they didn't get on so well," he shrugged.

"I'll get a pan out," she said stepping away. "Oh, and Ridge?"

"Yeah?" he asked his hand already on the doorknob.

"This makes me really happy," she smiled.
"Me too," he said before dashing back outside.

Chapter Twenty-Four

As the first official day of spring grew closer Leigha and Ridge developed a comfortable routine. They would spend their nights, and most of their mornings too, devouring each other. The heat always simmering between them never failing to ignite with merely a single touch. It amazed Leigha that with as much time they were spending burning up the sheets, it felt exciting each and every single time. Being in Ridge's arms never felt boring to her. A few times now Leigha found three particular little words sitting heavily on the tip of her tongue. For some reason they never made it past her lips, though Ridge told her all the time now how much he loved her. Each time he said it she felt it nestle a little deeper into her soul. This time with him was healing all the damage he left in his wake when he left at eighteen.

Tonight, they were having a movie night, each one of them picked a favorite movie to watch together. Ridge picked an action suspense movie that kept Leigha feeling like she was on the edge of her seat the whole time. Of course, she wasn't actually perched on the edge of her couch, she was curled into his side, with his arm around her shoulder keeping her tucked close. When the movie ended, he got up to let Boomer out to do his doggy business and make some popcorn in the microwave while she loaded up the next DVD into the player. The menu screen was on the television when he walked back into the living room, a giant bowl of fragrant buttery goodness in his hand. Boomer settled in the dog bed over in the corner Ridge left here for him, to nap with Finn who was already curled up there waiting for his furry friend.

"I figured you had some super sappy romance for us to watch. This is so much fucking better," Ridge said as a slow smile spread across his gorgeous face sending the butterflies in her middle into an excited frenzy.

"Well, this one's a classic, and still my favorite movie of all time," Leigha said with a grin, before adding, "We also spent more than a few times making out on your living room couch when your Mom was at work and we were supposed to be watching it. I figured maybe we're old enough now to get through the whole thing."

"Yeah, we barely made it past that opening song before we weren't paying attention anymore."

He laughed remembering back when they were younger. "Every time it came on TV I sat there watching it thinking about you. Hell, I've probably seen it more times than you have at this point," Ridge added as she hit the button on the remote.

Leigha almost choked on the popcorn she was enthusiastically munching when Ridge started singing along with the cast about summer nights. She swallowed carefully and although she knew that she was probably biased, Leigha thought he sounded even better than the voices floating out of the speakers. He wasn't exaggerating about how many times he'd seen it, he knew every single one of the words. His voice had always given her chills, right from the first time she heard it sitting across a bonfire from him. Now he was singing along to her all-time favorite movie, flawlessly, because throughout the years they were apart he had watched it thinking of her. As the song faded away and the movie moved on, he turned to her with a happy smile.

"I love you Ridge," she blurted out, surprising them both. Her mouth moved before her head had a chance to catch up, and maybe that's how it was meant to be all along. Because looking into his eyes right now she felt like the earth had stopped rotating. The endless green depths seemed to shimmer, and she watched the emotions surging through him as each one moved through his eyes.

"Finally," he breathed leaning until his forehead touched hers. "It's so damn good to hear you say that Leigha. I thought you were on the same page as I was, but I didn't know how bad I needed the actual words until now."

"They just came out before I even knew I was going to say them. I wasn't trying to hold out on you Ridge, I hope you know that," she said tunneling her fingers into his dark hair and pressing a whisper soft kiss against his lips.

Leigha felt him lifting the popcorn bowl out from his lap, where it was sitting, presumably setting it on the table next to the arm of the couch. She didn't really care where he set it, all she knew was that his lap was empty now and she needed to be in it. Keeping her hands in his hair she angled her body and lifted up, sliding one leg on each side of his, straddling him. His big hands gripped her hips grinding her down onto him. She could feel how hard he already was beneath her. Rolling her hips against him had heat pooling between her thighs, soaking into the panties she was wearing. Moaning into his mouth, already half crazed with need for him she reached between them and yanked the t shirt he was wearing up and over his head before sending it flying. Running her hands down his bared skin to the button of his jeans while she trailed hot kisses over the top of his shoulder. Leigha could feel the need pouring off Ridge, and it was fueling the blaze inside of her. His jeans undone she reached her hands inside of and wrapped her fingers around his dick at the same time she scraped her teeth along the side of his neck.

Ridge's growling intake of breath telling her exactly how much he liked what she was doing to him. "You've got too many clothes on Sugar."

Leigha nodded her head as she sucked his earlobe into her mouth. "Whatcha gonna do about it?"

His hands slid up her back bringing the shirt she was wearing with them. The callouses on his fingers from years of playing the guitar scraping her soft skin deliciously. He lifted it up over her head and tossed it. Reaching a hand up Ridge grabbed a handful of her long hair in his hand and tilted her head all the way to the side as he nibbled across her neck. Even when she was the one on top he was still in control, and she loved it. His other hand was busy unhooking her bra, sliding it off her body quickly.

Using the hand still in holding her hair he pulled down, and Leigha arched her back to accommodate. As she leaned back, he leaned in and caught her nipple and sucked it into his mouth. Shuddering over him Leigha closed her eyes, loving the way he always knew what she needed. Ridge released her hair and pushed her up off his lap. She stood there blinking at him for a second, her brain cells scrambling.

"Take your jeans off for me Sugar. Let me see all of your beautiful body," Ridge growled, lifting his hips and scooting his own jeans the rest of the way down his legs.

A smile stretching across her face Leigha ran her hands over her body. Feeling like a goddess standing in front of him, she watched the heat leap into his eyes as she palmed her breasts, before lightly pinching her nipples.

"Harder," he said.

Obeying without hesitation she squeezed down, her eyes locked on his.

"Fuck. Sugar, you like that don't you?" he asked already knowing the answer. "Twist those pretty pink nipples now."

Leigha twisted the nipples she was still holding pinched in between her thumb and pointer fingers. A low moan escaped her lips at the sensation.

"The clothes, lose them," Ridge said through gritted teeth.

With a final tug on her nipples, she smoothed her hands down to her waist. Leigha pulled the button free and dragged the zipper down feeling the zing of each one of the little teeth it passed over. Pushing her jeans and panties over her hips she stepped out of them, back towards Ridge. He held a hand up stopping her from climbing back onto his lap.

"Do you know what I've always wanted to see Sugar?" he asked her. Leigha shook her head back and forth. "I want to watch you make yourself come for me with just your fingers on that greedy pussy of yours."

Leigha gasped feeling his dirty words skate along her skin. Never in her whole life had she ever felt more wanted. Harnessing all of the sensations swirling inside of her she reached her hand down. She was so drenched it was dripping down her thighs as she reached between her lips and rubbed her throbbing clit with her fingertips. It felt so good she couldn't help but close her eyes. Leigha wasn't new to getting herself off, but doing it in front of Ridge like this, putting on a show just for him, had the familiar feel of her own fingers feeling more exciting than it ever had before.

Leigha heard Ridge demanding she open her eyes. It took two tries to peel her eyelids open, but when she managed to, the sight of him staring at her with such raw, abject hunger in his eyes had her gasping. Feeling bold she lifted a leg and set it on the edge of the couch, giving him an even better view as she pushed two fingers as deep inside of her pussy as she could reach. The angle had the advantage of the heel of her hand pressing into her clit as she rocked her hips into her hand. She saw moisture bead up on the tip of his dick, and knew he was enjoying the show. Rolling one of her nipples in between her fingers as she fucked herself for him. Ridge licked his lips, and lazily stroked himself with one hand, almost like he didn't realize he was even doing it. Her legs started shaking, as the pressure building inside of her reached its peak. Leigha's hips sped up, and she came moaning his name.

Ridge reached out grabbing her hips and pulling her down on top of him. Her aftershocks fluttering around his dick as it slid inside. He caught her wrist and lifted it up to his mouth, licking her fingers clean of the slick juices coating them.

"Mmmmm, you always taste so delicious," he groaned. "How did that feel?"

"So damn good," Leigha moaned.

"Want more?" Ridge asked with a sexy smirk.

"You know I do," she answered huskily.

"I'm all yours Sugar," he said grabbing her face in his hands and kissing her. She could still taste herself on his tongue, and it only turned her on even more.

Her hands gripping his arms, holding them to her, she started moving. Leigha knew she wouldn't last long, another orgasm already making the walls of her pussy tremble around him. Too far gone for slow, she rode him as fast as her hips would move, letting gravity slam her down onto him hard. Biting into his lip she felt his hips come up to meet hers with each thrust. In the background the movie still played, mingling with the sound of their bodies slapping hungrily into each other. She ripped her mouth away from his to let the moan bubbling up inside of her out. As the orgasm tore through her body she felt him swell and knew by the rush of heat he was right there with her. Leigha stayed there, on his lap, her whole body trembling from the force of the pleasure flowing through it.

"You love me," Ridge said, his voice betraying

all of the awe he was feeling.

"I really do," Leigha smiled. "And we still can't manage to sit and watch this movie."

Ridge's sexy laugh rumbled through the room as he stood up catching her ass in his hands and carried her off into the bedroom for more.

Chapter Twenty-Five

Leigha's phone rang as she was walking out of the bank the next day. Looking down at the display her whole face lit up in a blinding smile.

"Hey handsome," she answered.

"Hey Sugar. Remember how I was going to marinate some chops to throw on the grill for us tonight?" Ridge said sounding sheepish.

"I remember hearing mention of that. Let me guess, you forgot?" she laughed standing in the parking lot next to her car waving at one of her regulars as he walked past heading into the bank.

"Yeah. To my credit I've spent the majority of the day on the phone with my manager though," he said. "So I was thinking I could meet you at Borrello's and make a date of it?"

Leigha looked down at her Caffeinated Sprinkles shirt, noticing the smear of caramel syrup she was sporting right on the front. "Sounds good, meet you there in thirty?" She opened her door and climbed into her car. That gave her enough time to get home and change.

"I could pick you up," Ridge replied.

"Then you would just have to bring me back home for work at the crack of dawn." She started the car and pulled out heading the short distance home.

"Or I could spend the night at your place." She could hear the smile in his voice.

"Uh-uh, you said we could try out your newly installed hot tub tonight, and I've been looking forward to it all day long."

"Maybe we should skip the pizza place then," Ridge said with a playful growl.

"Not a chance. You're feeding me first Ridge Bradley, what kind of woman do you think I am?" Leigha said walking into her house. Finn immediately started weaving himself through her ankles. Leaning down she ran her hand from his head down his back to his tail.

"Good idea, you're going to need your energy. And you're my woman, that's what kind."

A delicious thrill tingled down her spine in anticipation. "Oh, is that so?"

"Hell yes it is, I can never get enough of you. Pack clothes for tomorrow babe, that way you won't have to get up so early and head home before work. See you in twenty-five minutes, and counting. Love you."

"Love you too," she whispered.

"Never get sick of hearing that Sugar," Ridge said before ending the call.

Leigha pulled the elastic out of her hair as she walked into her bedroom. Standing in front of her closet she tossed her dirty work clothes in the hamper over in the corner, and considered all of her options. Borrello's was just a little small-town pizzeria, the food was great, but most people didn't bother to dress up there. This was technically the first date they were having this time around, though. At least the first one somewhere out in public. She wanted to look good for her man, wanted to watch his gorgeous eyes taking all of her in from across the table. Her coral-colored shirt dress bridged the gap. It was chill enough that she wouldn't stand out like a sore thumb, but there was a casual sexiness to it that she thought Ridge would appreciate. Pulling it over her head she spent a few minutes fiddling with the buttons down the front, so he would get a sneaky peek-a-boo of her cleavage, before adding a brown leather belt at her waist. She tossed some clothes in a tote for work tomorrow, and slipped her feet into cognac colored ankle boots.

Walking into the bathroom she decided what the hell. In for a penny, in for a pound. Opening the drawer, she pulled out her seldom used makeup bag. Adding a couple swipes of mascara to her top lashes, and a slick of lip gloss to her mouth. She had to kneel down to look under the sink for the bottle of sea salt spray the stylist talked her into during her last haircut. Giving the bottle a quick shake, she spritzed it all over and sort of scrunched her hair in her hands like the girl told her to. One enthusiastic shake, and her thick brown hair settled around her head, making her think of *just fucked* hair, and hoping Ridge got the same image in his mind when he saw it.

Checking the time, she walked back into the kitchen and gave Finn enough food to keep him happy until tomorrow when she got home from work. She picked him up and scratched behind his ears. "See you later Finn, don't throw any wild parties while I'm gone, honey," she said giving his sweet face a quick nuzzle.

Setting him back down she plucked her dark wash denim jacket off the hook and maneuvered her arms awkwardly into it while trying not to set her purse and overnight bag down. Laughing at herself she stepped into the garage, locking the door behind her. She leaned into the car setting her bags on the passenger seat before slipping in. Leigha caught a glimpse of her reflection in the mirror as she pulled out of the driveway and smiled.

The drive across town only took her five minutes before she was parking next to his big truck, already sitting there waiting for her. She was just closing the door when Ridge stepped out of his truck. He was wearing a charcoal gray henley with a pair of dark jeans. She saw the initials RB worked into the intricate design of his belt buckle, since his shirt was caught behind it. He stopped an arm's length away from her, and his eyes swept her from the toes up. She felt his gaze travel along her body and reveled in it. When his eyes finally met hers there was enough heat swirling in them, she wondered how there weren't curls of smoke leaking out of his ears. He set his hand on the side of her neck, his thumb brushing softly along her jaw.

"Damn, baby. You walk in there looking like that nobody's gonna be able to keep their eyes in their heads. I sure am a lucky bastard, that I'm the one who gets your heart." There was a smirk on his face, but his eyes betrayed the depth of what he was saying. "Come on, I wanna show you off," he added catching her hand in his and leading the way across the parking lot towards Borrello's.

"Ridge, I grew up here too. Everybody in there

already knows what I look like," Leigha said laughing.

"Doesn't mean a damn thing Sugar," Ridge said as he pulled the door open for her.

Borrello's did a good business between the delivery, carry out, and dining room. Ridge steered her past the small to-go counter to the hostess stand. Leigha recognized the girl standing there with a big smile lighting up her face, she liked brownies, and an extra shot of espresso in her latte.

"Welcome to Borrello's, let me show you to a table," she said in a nervous rush. She walked into the dining room towards a circular table covered in a red checkered tablecloth off to the side. "How's this table?" she asked.

"Perfect, thank you," Ridge said with a knowing smile. He held the chair out for Leigha, before walking over to his own.

Their hostess's hands were shaking when she set the menus down in front of them. "Kevin, umm, he's gonna be your waiter tonight, he will be along shortly," she turned bright red and hurried back to the front of the restaurant.

"Is it always like that?" Leigha asked as she watched the girl. "She was so excited she could barely speak, then mortified that she wasn't cool and collected."

"Not always, but it happens a lot, yeah," Ridge said with a shrug. "It's better than the people who forget I'm an actual person."

"What do you mean?" Leigha asked picking up her menu. She didn't really need it though. She had eaten everything on it at least once in her life.

"Like when you're just trying to take a piss and a woman barges into the men's room with her phone up and ready to snap a picture of your dick. Or when people tell me how much they hated my song in the grocery store. And every time I'm sitting at a bar that means I'm gonna get asked to sing my songs." He sighed. "I get it. I signed up for this life, and that means I opened myself up to that. But I'm not just a product ya know. Sometimes I just want to be just a person."

Just then Kevin showed up to take their order. Ridge decided on the lasagna, and Leigha went with fettuccine alfredo. Neither of them were apparently in the mood for pizza. Once Kevin walked away Leigha returned to the subject.

"Is that why you wanted to come home?" she asked him resting her head in her hand.

"It definitely factored in there, yeah. But mostly, I missed you Leigha. I tried to move on, and failed fucking miserably at it. I just couldn't stay away anymore," he said reaching across the table for her hand. Leigha immediately laid her palm against his.

"When you say things like that I forget how to breathe," she said honestly.

"I'm not gonna lie, I really like knowing I do that to you," he said with a big grin reminding her of how he used to look before he left, and life got in the way. There was such an uncomplicated ease in that.

Kevin walked over and set their drinks down letting them know their food would be ready in a few minutes.

"Well, our waiter doesn't seem to be too impressed with you, he barely looked your way," Leigha said.

"To see me he would have to peel his eyes off you, and he isn't about to do that. Don't blame him though. When you're in a room there isn't anywhere else worth looking." His thumb was making lazy circles over her knuckles.

"Guess I didn't notice. My focus was elsewhere," Leigha said, her voice husky.

Ridge leaned forward. "I know."

Leigha felt the heat pooling in her center, and knew that if the food didn't show up in the next thirty seconds she was going to stand up and drag him out of here. Crossing her legs, she squeezed her thighs together and tried not to think about how fast they could make it out to his truck. She could tell by the slow simmer in his eyes that Ridge knew where her thoughts had gone.

Kevin walked up just then and set their plates down in front of them. He said something, before walking away again. Neither one of them heard him, so lost in each other.

"Come on Sugar, you said I had to feed you. You keep looking at me like that and I'm not going to be able to hold myself back."

Desire written all over her face Leigha pulled her hand out of his and picked up her fork. "I'll do my best. Although, I might not mind that," she added just to watch the sexy smile break across his face. "So, how come you were on the phone all day? Is everything okay?" Leigha asked as she swirled her fork in the noodles before taking a bite.

"Yeah, it's all good. Just trying to get everything arranged," Ridge said staring at her mouth.

"For what?" Leigha asked as she slowly licked a bit of sauce off her bottom lip.

"Huh?" Ridge asked distracted.

"What were you arranging with your manager?" Leigha asked with a knowing smile. It made her feel good that she could completely blank out his mind so easily. This was a man who could have just about any woman he wanted to, but he was all hers.

"Oh yeah." Ridge laughed, "The ACM's are this month. I'm supposed to perform, and I'm up for an award."

"That's awesome Ridge!" Leigha said, proud of him. "I'll be cheering you on this year," she said, not adding that in years previous she avoided watching the awards shows like the plague. Hearing about which awards he won always made her so proud, but that didn't mean she could handle watching. Seeing his face on the screen was just too hard. It never failed to remind her of the aching emptiness in her heart where he was supposed to be. Things were different now though. With Ridge back in her life, there was no reason to avoid them.

"I was actually hoping you could come with me Leigha," Ridge said quietly. The intensity in his eyes betraying just how much her being there meant to him.

"Oh, Ridge, I don't think I can. Who will run Caffeinated Sprinkles?" she said feeling like a dream killer.

"Didn't you just give Tina more responsibilities?" he asked.

"Yeah, we are doing well enough, and I was hoping to be able to get a day off every now and again."

"Between her and Dani couldn't they manage?"

"How long would I be gone?" Leigha asked, her mind running through all the possibilities.

"A week. I have rehearsals, and there are press and events to attend leading up to it." Ridge answered.

She could see the hope burning in his eyes. "Do I have to answer tonight? I'd like to talk this through with Dani tomorrow, and see if Tina is up for it."

Ridge nodded. "Yeah, let me know if it's something you can swing. It would mean a lot to me having you by my side."

"So Ridge, I've been fed. What do you say we get out of here?" Leigha asked, determined to turn the conversation around again.

"I was ready to leave before we walked in." Ridge set some cash on the table, enough to cover the bill plus the tip, and stood up with a scrape of his chair. He held his hand out to Leigha. "Come on, let's go break my hot tub in."

Chapter Twenty-Six

The temperatures hadn't been warm enough for Leigha to spend much time out on Ridge's back deck yet. Taking a step out the door to watch Boomer run around the yard, or urinate on every single blade of grass available, hardly counted. A massive thing, it stretched across the whole back of the house. Outside the French door just off the kitchen a couple steps led down to the grass where the yard had a gradual slope to accommodate the walk out basement. Further down, the deck sat much higher off the ground, and there was even a patio with a built-in fire pit which you could access from the basement.

There was a comforting softness to the darkness surrounding them, the tree line a few yards away was hazy and indistinct. Solar lights mounted atop the railing gave the whole porch a warm flickering glow. The ground was a ways down on this side of the deck, adding to the air of privacy, not that it was necessary since Ridge didn't have any neighbors living close by. Eight people would have had enough room to sit and relax in the hot tub, and never worry about touching each other if they didn't want to. Steam was already rising up from the surface of the water to dance seductively in the cool evening air.

The smile on Leigha's face was decidedly sexy as she turned away from the hot tub and faced Ridge. Snaking her hands around his neck she pressed herself against all the hard angles of his body she loved so very much. Pressing a kiss to the base of his neck, just above the collar of his cotton shirt she whispered, "I've been thinking about this all day." His arms came around her, fingers gripping her ass as he pulled her hips even closer. She could feel how hard he was even through the material of his jeans, and her dress. Leigh rubbed herself shamelessly up against him while she waited to hear his response.

"Have you been wet and aching the whole time too?" he asked leaning in to take her mouth in a devastating kiss. He pushed the denim jacket off her shoulders, and let it fall onto the wooden boards under their feet. "This hair looks like I've fucked you a few times already."

"I wanted you to look at me across the table and think about how much you want your hands in my hair," Leigha said lifting his shirt up and over his head.

"I've always loved your hair. It's so thick and dark, but if you watch it in the sunlight there are a dozen different shades of bronze shooting through it," he said taking a handful of it to tip her head back. Licking up the side of her neck he said, "And you fucking love it when I pull it while I'm deep inside of you."

Leigha moaned and reached up inside of his shirt and scraped her nails across his skin. Just the sound of his voice was enough to take her there. She was addicted to him, her whole body tingling in greedy anticipation. "I really do."

Ridge reached between them and she could feel his fingers freeing the buttons on the front of her dress, pushing it down her shoulders. The sheer peach lace bra offering no defense against the night air caressing her skin. "God, to think you had this on under your dress the whole time we sat in that restaurant. This ripe color against all of this creamy skin, it's enough to make my mouth water," he said reverently, as he cupped her full breasts, his thumbs brushing back and forth across her nipples. Just when her head fell back to absorb what his hands were doing to her, he moved them. Before Leigha could voice a protest, she felt him pulling the belt off her waist. With nothing left to hold it up the gauzy fabric drifted lazily down her body. He peppered kisses over the top of her shoulder whispering, "I used to jerk off thinking about these freckles here. Remember that purple bikini you used to have? The one with the little pink stripes?"

Leigha's head was spinning from the swing back and forth between the dirty words and the romantic ones. Just when she settled in, he switched the tone again. It was sweet torment. "I had that one when I was fifteen, that was the summer before we started dating, Ridge."

"You and Dani used to lay out towels in her yard, soaking up the sun and listening to music," Ridge said, as he used his arms around her to tip her back so he could lick and nibble her collarbone. "I rode my bike past her house every damn day that summer, desperate to catch a glimpse of you."

Straightening abruptly she stared in his eyes with awe. "You did? I didn't know that."

"I've always wanted you Leigha, as long as I can remember," Ridge admitted.

Grabbing the intricate belt buckle she pulled his belt off. It made a soft whooshing sound as it cleared each of the loops in his jeans before she dropped it with a thud. Reeling from what he just said Leigha's patience was gone. She needed him now. Pushing down, both his jeans and his boxers she wrapped her hand around him as his dick bobbed out, free. She pumped him eagerly, dragging her thumb across the sensitive tip on every downstroke. Dropping to her knees in front of him, not giving a damn about the unforgiving wood under her she dragged her tongue up from the side of his knee. She looked up into his eyes as she closed her mouth around his dick. Leigha could barely close her lips around him, he was so wide. She worked just the head at first, swirling her tongue, varying her movements so he couldn't anticipate what sensation was going to hit him next.

Leigha watched his eyes drift closed, and she surged forward until her lips were against his body. Ridge's hands flew onto the back of her head, as he hunched forward. She worked her throat swallowing him down. She moved her head back taking a breath, and then forward again quickly.

Leigha pulled him against her face as she moved. His fingers gripped her hair hard on reflex, but the little bit of pain in her scalp only added to the moment.

"Holy mother-fucking shit. That feels....fuck," Ridge tried saying as she worked him. His hips were instinctively pumping now, his need overwhelming his control.

Riding high on the power coursing through her she grabbed his muscular ass in her hands and pulled her head back. Ridge's dick slid out of her mouth with a popping sound. She waited until his eyes opened and met hers. "I need more," she said. He leaned down to hook his hands under her arms and lift her back up to her feet. Leigha shook her head. "No. I mean, I want you to fuck my face just like this Ridge. I want to feel your control snap, and know that I did that to you. That you feel so good you can't think anymore."

His thumb stroked across her cheek bone. "Are you sure what you're asking for Sugar?"

Leigha nodded her head. "Yes." She watched as the heat blazing in his eyes exploded. His thumb moved down from her cheek to her mouth. He traced the shape of her lips, and she licked out, catching his thumb.

She opened her mouth and looked up at him, waiting. Ridge didn't disappoint, using the hand that was on her face to feed his dick into her mouth. Leigha slid her hands back around to his ass, as both of his threaded back into her hair. When he was all the way in, she swallowed, and the hands that were struggling to stay gentle in her hair gripped hard. He thrust his hips, his eyes locked on hers. Leigha watched him suck his bottom lip in, biting it as he picked up speed. The only breaths she could take were quick puffs through her nose as he pulled back. There was too much saliva pooling in her mouth to hold, and she let it flow out, dribbling down her chin.

"Fuck, you look so gorgeous taking my dick like that Sugar," he said.

His thrusts were getting erratic, and she knew he was getting close. Encouraging him to take all the pleasure she could offer, she rubbed her tongue against him as he pumped into her mouth.

"Close, I'm so god-damn close," he groaned, panting. "You're gonna swallow every fucking drop I give you, aren't you?"

Leigha couldn't speak with her mouth so full of Ridge, so she dug her nails into his ass, and moaned. That was all it took before he growled loudly into the night. He came in a warm gush down her throat. Leigha swallowed as fast as she could to keep up. Ridge was still trembling when he pulled out of her mouth. Leigha licked her lips savoring his taste and wiped the back of her hand across her face, as she stood up. He sagged against her, and she thought he needed her support to hold him upright, but one of his hands was unhooking her bra, and the other was yanking her lace boy-shorts down her hips.

"Was that what you needed?" Ridge's rough voice sounded like it was filled with gravel.

Leigha nodded. "You seemed to like it too baby."

He laughed. "Because I'm not an idiot. My woman wanted me to fuck her face, that's literally every man's fantasy." Ridge walked her backwards until her legs pressed against the hot tub. "Do you know what I want now?"

Leigha smiled and shook her head. "No, but I'm gonna love every second of it."

"I'll show you," Ridge said as grabbed her by the hips and lifted her into the hot tub. The water was warm, but not as hot as she was expecting. He must have read the confusion on her face. "I didn't want to burn that amazing pussy of yours while I was fucking it." Leigha's nipples pebbled hard, and it had nothing to do with the cool night air.

He stepped into the hot tub with her, and sat down. Leigha moved to sit next to him, but he pulled her onto his lap. Smiling she wove her fingers into his hair. Ridge leaned forward and caught one of her nipples in his teeth and gave a slight tug. Her surprised gasp ended in a moan as his tongue swept out to swirl the sensitive peak. The humidity from the rising steam had her hair curling wildly as she stared up at the stars. Ridge reached down, and teased her clit. He wasn't pressing hard enough to get her off, and he knew it. She rocked against him trying to ease the building ache inside. Laughing, he slipped one finger inside of her pussy, and stroked as he turned to her other nipple. Her thighs started shaking as she got closer and closer to the edge. He added a second finger and curled them against her g-spot. Leigha was so tantalizingly close.

"Come for me Leigha. I need to feel you break apart," Ridge said sucking on the underside of her breast.

Leigha knew that when she looked tomorrow that she would see his marks there. She wanted to see evidence of him all over her body. He knew his words would work, shoving her into the orgasm she was desperately reaching for. Her back arched, and she milked his hand as she came with a sobbing moan. His fingers didn't stop moving inside of her though, and she was struggling to pull air into her lungs.

"Again," he said, pressing until the heel of his palm ground against her clit.

Her first orgasm was barely over and he was dragging her up again. When she came a second time, he sat up quickly, and turned them. Setting Leigha on her knees he grabbed her hips and thrust inside from behind. Her pussy was still pulsing greedily from the two orgasms. The warm water around her had her feeling deliciously boneless. He pushed her front flush against the side of the hot tub, and Leigha felt him lean away. She turned to look back at him, and he sent her a wink as the jets came to life. There was one right between her legs, which he must have felt while he was sitting there moments earlier. He reached down and pulled her outer lips apart, and the powerful water beat mercilessly against her sensitive, throbbing nub as he pumped in and out of her.

Leigha gasped out a breathless, "Oh my god Ridge.....that's....oh my god." There was so much pleasure assaulting her body that at first it felt like too much. But she stopped fighting it and let go. Ridge bit down, not quite hard enough to break the skin, on the freckles he loved so much on her shoulder, and a ragged scream ripped out of her. It felt like the best orgasm of her life that just rolled continually on. If anyone heard her they would think she was being murdered, but she just didn't care.

There was no room inside of her for inhibitions with him. Her body was alive with sensations. Her pussy was squeezing his dick hard with each powerful thrust. He was fucking her hard enough that the water was splashing furiously all around them, as his body slammed into hers. She heard him yell, as he stilled behind her, his own intense orgasm exploding out of him.

Ridge reached back and turned the jets off, and Leigha collapsed exhaustedly over the side. She was completely certain that there were no bones left in her body, and she had never felt better. "You've ruined me for life," she said smiling as he plopped down next to her.

"I've got jets in the tub upstairs Sugar," he chuckled. "As soon as I find my legs, we can try them out too."

"There's no rush Ridge. It's gonna take hours before my clit recovers," she said kissing his shoulder.

Chapter Twenty-Seven

Being with Ridge was so intense that Leigha was still feeling it the next day. Her body felt generously, sinfully loose, like it was buzzing from the inside out the next morning. After they managed to make it out of the hot tub it was all they could do to crawl up the stairs and collapse in an exhausted heap curled up in his soft bed. As soon as Ridge wrapped his arms around her, she was out like a light. Leigha didn't even stir until the alarm went off across the room with a loud beeping, and she was grateful for it since she forgot her phone downstairs. It was still tucked inside her purse sitting on the dining room table where she left it on her way through the house last night. She stumbled out of bed turning it off on her way to the bathroom. The shower helped clear the haziness of sleep from her mind, but it did nothing to diminish the glow emanating from her.

Now standing inside of her shop taking a sip of the superb coffee she sold to customers all day long Leigha knew she didn't want to let Ridge go to that awards show alone. This place meant a lot to her, but so did he. If there was a way to have both then she was damn sure hoping to find it. She could admit to herself that she had held onto this place with a vise like, iron grip simply because it was all she had. Sure she had family, her parents, Dani and Silas. But at the end of the day she went home all alone. Caffeinated Sprinkles wasn't just a dream, it had turned into her coping mechanism for the gaping loneliness, when she felt like she had nothing else going for her. They could afford to hire more help, allow her to take a step back from the counter, probably for some time now. She just wasn't ready to consider the possibilities of that sooner.

When Dani walked in for the day Leigha was ready. She waited until Dani had the cookies going before she walked slowly back into the kitchen, gathering her thoughts with each step.

"Hey, I'm running on about five minutes of sleep, so if you came back here to tell me about your amazing sex life I'll take a pass today," Dani said brushing a hand across her brow. She sounded exhausted, and not the kind that comes only from lack of sleep.

"What happened Dani?" Leigha asked walking next to her friend and wrapping an arm around her. Dani immediately leaned into the comforting warmth of a decades long friendship.

"It was just normal stuff really. I had a headache and didn't want to cook anything, so I tossed some pizza's in the oven. Normally Silas loves it, but last night he wasn't impressed with it at all. Then he got an attitude with me at bedtime, and I ended up yelling at him. Which I felt like crap about it the rest of the night and couldn't sleep. He seemed no worse for wear this morning, but nights like that I really wish I wasn't the only one around ya know? It would be nice to know there was someone else I could count on to help," Dani said, bringing her hands up to swipe errant tears away. "I didn't think I would be doing this alone when I got pregnant."

"I'm sorry Jason is a monumental asshole Dani. You and Silas really deserve better. Last night sounds like it was tough, but you really are a great mom. Don't doubt that, ever. Nobody is perfect all the time, my parents stayed married, happily I might add, and my Mom snapped at me once or twice growing up. I turned out alright. Silas will too. You're only human, you are allowed to have a bad night once in a while." Leigha took a deep breath. "I've been thinking about our workload, and I think it's time you and I give ourselves a break. Tina is full time now, and I want to find someone to help you out here in the kitchen full time. In fact, I think we need to hire another part time person too."

Dani pulled away from Leigha and stared at her. "You do? Oh, thank god, me too. This place is doing so well, but it's getting kind of hard to keep up."

"Alright, it's settled then. Tina should be here in a few minutes, and I will get on making an advertisement to put online. I'll also get a sign in the front window. I've got another chalkboard tucked away in the office that I can use for that. To think I was going to talk to you about going to Nashville for a week soon, but you definitely need some time off much more than I do." Leigha turned to leave the kitchen, wheels already in motion.

"Hold on. Wait just a damn minute," Dani said, using her Mom voice, and it halted Leigha dead in her tracks. "Did Ridge ask you to go there with him?"

Leigha nodded, feeling guilty. "Yeah, he has something he needs to be there for, an awards show he is slated to perform at."

"Awards? Shit, Leigha he's talking about the Academy of Country Music Awards isn't he?"

"Yeah," Leigha said.

"You have to go!" Dani all but shouted with

excitement.

"No, we need me here so you can get a breather," Leigha argued digging her heels in. "I'll go with him to the next awards, these things roll around quite regularly."

"Oh, shut up! I appreciate you thinking of me first, but honestly even if we hired an assistant baker this afternoon I wouldn't be able to entrust them with the whole kitchen for a while. Tina already knows what she is doing, she's got it handled. Hell, you've spent half the day back in the office lately, and she never needs to call you out to help up front. Now, your man, the one you have been ass over head in love with since you were sixteen years old wants you by his side for this. It's probably really important to him, and he wants to share that part of his life with you because he's been in love with you just as long. You're going, and don't you dare say another word about it!" Dani ended her speech with a decisive nod that sent her ponytail swaying.

"I really love you Dani. Honestly, it takes talent to make me feel all giddy inside while you're chewing my ass out," Leigha said, her cheeks turning up in a smile as she sighed. "If you think this place can handle my absence then I guess I'm out of excuses."

"Damn right you are, Finn can come over for the week too. Silas will love helping take care of him. Now get out of my kitchen so I can get these cookies out front. You've got an ad to put together, and a sign to make." Dani shooed Leigha away with a laugh.

Leigha was walking out of the kitchen, feeling like everything was falling into place as Tina breezed in for the day.

"Good morning boss lady." Tina smiled as she stashed her purse in the little alcove under the counter for them. "You look like you're in a good mood."

"It definitely is a good morning, and I really am. I wanted to let you know how happy I am with how you've handled the transition to full time. I guess I shouldn't have waited so long, you've got this down," Leigha said watching as Tina tied her navy apron with the *CS* logo in mint green on the front, around her waist. "We're planning on hiring a full-time assistant baker to help Dani out, and probably a part timer for out here as well."

"That's great, this is a really cool place to work, I'm sure you'll get tons of applications in no time," Tina said as she readied for the day signing into the computer system on the cash register.

"Thanks, fingers crossed," Leigha said smiling as she started down the short hallway.

"And toes too!" Tina shouted enthusiastically at her.

Leigha was laughing as she walked into her office and shut the door.

Chapter Twenty-Eight

At least twenty applications sat in a neat stack on her desk by the end of the day. Word that Caffeinated Sprinkles was hiring had swiftly spread like a wave crashing through the entire town. There were a dozen more waiting for Leigha in her email inbox from the advertisement she posted online too. Giving her chair a spin, she swirled around the office throwing her head back and laughing, just as Dani walked in. Leigha spotted her friend and business partner leaning against the door jamb smiling. Setting her foot down she halted the circular motion of her office chair.

"Last time I walked in to see you doing that was that first month we actually turned a profit," Dani said caught up in Leigha's unencumbered joy. "I take it we have some decent applicants in that stack?"

"We sure do. I honestly wish we could hire half of them on the spot. Coffee shop experience, check. Bakery experience, check. References, check," she said pulling applications from the stack and waving them around excitedly. "And, that's just right here. I haven't even finished reading the online ones yet! So, hell yes I'm pretty excited!"

Dani walked over and quickly scanned through the papers. She nodded setting two of them aside. "I like these two, forward me any of the promising bakers from your inbox. I'll call them in for interviews." Dani paused, her head slightly tilted to the side. "Did you ever think we would get here?" She gestured with her hands and added, "I mean, I know we dreamed it, sure. But I kind of wondered if it would always just be the two of us holding the place together through sheer will and stubbornness."

"To be honest, I wouldn't have even thought about it. This place was everything to me, my whole life, and working day in and day out, until I fell into bed completely exhausted, suited me just fine," Leigha admitted. "Now, I want to have it all. I want to grow our business, but I also want a life. I want us both to have more to our lives."

Dani nodded wisely. "Seems to me like you might just have it all already, you just have to let yourself." When Leigha nodded Dani pulled away from the doorway. "I'm gonna take Silas to see that new super hero movie tonight. We need a night out. He's been talking about it for weeks. He can geek out on the action, and I'll stuff my face full of popcorn and call it a win. Catch you later." She tapped the applications against her hand with a grin before walking out.

Leigha combed through her email quickly, sending two more of them Dani's way. She had a list of five people to interview for up front, and Dani had four tentatively to help in the kitchen. Feeling pretty good about it she worked her way down the list calling people back for interviews. Locking up she took the deposit to the bank. The late afternoon sun was shining brightly, even if the air was still just this side of chilly. It didn't matter, in Michigan if the sun was shining it was a good day. Winter was long, gray, and perpetually dreary. Spring's arrival not only woke the spindly looking trees up from their long nap, it brought some much needed light back to people's faces. Leigha stood next to her car, her face tilted up towards the warm rays, and closed her eyes. Inhaling, she absorbed the joy drifting through the light. Her life was falling into place in ways she wouldn't have thought possible last season, and she was ready to embrace it

"Love sure does look good on you, my dear," Mrs. Bowman said, surprising Leigha. "I am glad Ridge tore down that silly wall you spent all those years building."

Too damn happy to bother being embarrassed Leigha opened her eyes and grinned at the retired teacher. "Thanks, I am too."

"I always knew that boy would be back," Mrs. Bowman added.

"Really?"

"Absolutely, always," Mrs. Bowman repeated with a decisive nod.

"Why's that?" Leigha asked, her face filling with confusion.

"Even back then it was plain for anyone with eyes to see, you two were just meant. Growing up the way he did, a boy without a father he had a fire inside of him burning to make something of himself. If he had stayed, I don't think either one of you would have found the happiness I can see pouring out of you now. He needed to show himself he was worthy," Mrs. Bowman said giving Leigha's hand a pat that could only be described as grandmotherly.

"Ridge was always worth it to me." Leigha said softly.

"Yes, dear, I'm sure he was. It takes some men awhile to catch up though."

"He told me that he never stopped loving me, the whole time he was gone. Even through his whole marriage," Leigha found herself admitting, the words slipping out before she could think twice.

"I've no doubt he was telling you the God's honest truth." Mrs. Bowman nodded sagely. "Feelings that deep don't ever go away, even if you want them to."

"He was married. He had a wife," Leigha said. That was something that still bothered her, how could he love her and marry another woman.

"Doesn't that make you wonder what that must have cost his soul, saying those vows to another?" she said squeezing Leigha's hand. "Well, I've got to get going, some of the girls are coming over tonight to play cards." With a wiggle of her brows she walked off to her car a couple spaces away.

Leigha thought about that as she watched Mrs. Bowman pull out of the parking lot. She was jealous of Suzy, sure. Who wouldn't be? She would always have a part of Ridge that Leigha never could. That was easy to admit to herself as she finally sat down in her car. Maybe a tiny part of her still worried Ridge would decide Suzy was who he wanted after all. After hearing what Mrs. Bowman had to say on the matter Leigha just wasn't sure anymore. The older woman was a fountain of wisdom to be sure. She was practically an institution in their small town for a reason. It was definitely going to take some time for Leigha to digest what she had told her.

Leigha's phone rang as she was pulling up into her driveway. Putting her car in park Leigha leaned over and dug through the contents of her purse. Pulling it out she answered it moments before it would have dumped the caller into her voicemail greeting.

"Hey," Leigha said quickly.

"Hey Sugar. How was your day?" She could hear the smile in his voice, and just that had her body already tingling with need.

"Pretty good. I set up some interviews for tomorrow, so I'm really hoping Caffeinated Sprinkles will be growing pretty soon," Leigha said letting her head tip back into the seat.

"You sound a little nervous about that," Ridge said.

"Not so much nervous, as ready to be there already. I want the interviews over. Now that we are taking this step I just want it done with. I honestly can't wait until I can schedule myself some days off. Which is something I never thought I would say."

"So I take it Dani was on board with the whole thing?" he asked, his deep voice sounding so damn warm but with a powerful punch that went straight to your gut, just like good whiskey.

Leigha was so caught up listening to the way Ridge's voice ebbed and flowed through her mind that she lost the thread of what he was saying. "Leigha?" she heard. "You still with me babe?"

"Always. I was just enjoying the sound of your voice," Leigha purred, and then rushed on, "Yeah, it turns out that Dani needed the help too. She always makes juggling work and time with Silas look so effortless, that apparently even I was fooled. She is probably even happier about this whole thing than I am."

"I'm on my way over," Ridge said. She could hear him moving around his house quickly.

"Wait, what? I thought you were going to try and get some writing done tonight?" Leigha asked confused.

"You think I didn't catch what you said Sugar?"

"Which part?" Leigha asked struggling to catch up replaying her words back in her head.

"You lost what I was saying because you were just listening to me," Ridge explained. Leigha heard the distinctive sound of his front door shutting.

"Well you do have quite a voice Ridge, it's

kind of well documented by now. I'm not the only woman who enjoys the sound of it."

"No, you're not. But you don't realize how you sounded, do you? Your voice got all low and smoky just like it does when I'm inside you. Which means that I'm rock hard right now, and I'm thinking that the only song I'd be writing tonight is not one they will be able to play on country radio." Leigha heard his truck start up.

"I'll be waiting," Leigha said rushing into her house.

"Damn right you will," Ridge all but growled as he hung up the phone.

Chapter Twenty-Nine

Time flew by so fast that the days felt like one blurred into the next until the whole week was one continuous wave. Training new employees was always as interesting as it was challenging. Leigha was trying to remember all the little things that were second nature to her by now. Every night when she finally closed her eyes a million things she was absolutely sure she had forgotten to explain assaulted her tired brain. She would toss and turn for hours before the relentless exhaustion claimed her. In a moment she thought was pure genius, she threw together a training manual, sent to Dani to look over and add anything she could think of. The next time Caffeinated Sprinkles hired new people they would be one hundred percent covered, or at least that was the plan. The four new employees, two front counter, and two back in the kitchen brought them officially up to a staff of seven.

It took Leigha less time than she would have thought to be comfortable with the changes though. Her Mom stopped by for a bite, meaning a bit of chat, Friday morning. Leigha was able to sit with her Mom at one of their cute little tables without running back behind the counter every few minutes to help customers. It was glorious.

"I've already got my DVR set to record the awards, you know. Your Dad is telling everyone who will listen that his baby girl is going to be on the TV," her Mom said as she sipped her coffee.

"I highly doubt that you will even see me Mom," Leigha said laughing. "I'm just his date, nobody special."

"Really, darling? Do you honestly think that nobody will be paying attention to who he has on his arm? I know to you he is just Ridge, but to a whole lot of people he is *the* Ridge Bradley country music superstar extraordinaire. Speculation is already running rampant. His ex-wife is performing too which has the rumor mill in a right tizzy already." Leigha's Mom gently grabbed her hand and added, "Not to mention this will be your first foray into that part of his life."

"Way to make me even more nervous than I already was Mom," Leigha muttered.

"I figured you might be, this is a big step, and you haven't been back together very long."

"To have Ridge in *my* life I have to accept all

that comes with *his* life," Leigha said, repeating the mantra that had been on a constant loop inside of her head ever since she had agreed to be his date at the award show.

"Yes, you do. But that doesn't mean you're going to immediately like it, and that's alright. Being famous was never one of your dreams." Her Mom looked outside lost in thought a moment. "Ridge was though. He was woven into every single plan you had for your future. This isn't about all the glitz and the glam, as fun as I'm sure it will be. You're going in support of your man, and honey Ridge is yours, heart and soul. Some women have to smile pretty at company dinners next to their men, this is basically the same thing, albeit on a much grander scale."

"He keeps telling me how happy he is that I'm coming with him. He does this all the time, but I'm starting to get the impression he is just as nervous as I am this time," Leigha confided.

"Of course he is. You said that he told you he knew it wasn't right with Suzy. This is the big reveal. He is showing the world, at least his corner of it, who he really is inside," her mom said with a smile.

"I guess I didn't think of it like that, but you're right. Bringing me is basically pinning his heart on his sleeve for everyone to see. What if it doesn't go the way he hopes Mom?" Leigha said working the end of her long braid through her fingertips nervously.

"Neither one of you have control over everything. I'm sure there will be people who don't think you should be with him, who think he shouldn't have divorced Suzy. And plenty of people who just want him single forever so they think there is a chance for them. You can't worry about any of that. Your job is to make him feel how much he means to you, same as it's his job to show you how important you are to him. Do you remember that summer he sang a couple of songs at the fair? He spent weeks rehearsing, while you printed up posters and hung them all over town. Everyone knew Ridge was singing because you told them they didn't want to miss it. You supported him then, this is the same thing. Instead of plastering posters everywhere you're going to be wearing a beautiful dress and walking the red carpet by his side."

"He dedicated the show to me that night," Leigha said losing herself in the memory of how that had felt back then.

Seventeen years old, filled with so much love and pride she could have lit up the night sky so bright you would think it was mid-day. Leigha stood there with all their friends watching Ridge swagger across the stage to the microphone. He smiled right down at her and said with a wink, "This is for my girl, without her none of you would probably even be here." A laugh went across the crowd, but the background noise faded away as Ridge started to play. All Leigha saw was Ridge.

"While everyone else was looking up at the stage, I only saw you. The look on your face as you watched him, well it will stay with me forever," she said with a shake of her head and a sigh. "Don't you worry about the awards. Just enjoy getting to know this part of Ridge, and enjoy being with him."

"Thanks, Mom. I'll try," Leigha said as her Mom stood up to go. She wrapped her arms around her and hugged tight.

Later that night Leigha was sitting in Dani's living room waiting for her friend to come back from kissing Silas goodnight. Dani looked tired but happy as she walked out, shutting the door behind her softly. Leigha waiting to speak until Dani sat down on the couch and had a chance to take a sip of her wine.

"Well? How do you think this week went?" Leigha asked.

Dani laughed. "Just about jumping out of

your skin with impatience aren't you?"

"I thought I was holding it together quite nicely actually," Leigha said sticking her nose up in the air a moment before the laugh bubbled up her throat. "Okay, patience was never my strongest attribute."

"Nope. Definitely down there somewhere near the bottom of the list," Dani replied laughing too. "As exhausting as it's been for us, I think it went better than I expected. All four of the new hires are working out. I was a little worried that we would end up with at least one dud in the bunch."

"Me too actually. But they all got it," Leigha said tucking her legs comfortably underneath her.

"They really do. I'm already mentally planning my first day off. I'm gonna drop Silas off at school then spend the rest of my day taking a gloriously uninterrupted nap," Dani said with an exaggerated sigh.

"You would be bored within five minutes, and you know it." Leigha said.

"Probably. It's a damn nice fantasy though." Dani leaned back further into the cushions. "But in all seriousness, I think we got it handled Leigha."

"I was almost hoping that it wouldn't work out," Leigha admitted with a tiny shrug.

"Yeah, I know. But that's only because you know once you take this step with Ridge the two of you are all but written in stone," Dani said gently.

"Which really shouldn't bother me. We have said the *I love you's* again," Leigha said, her teeth nervously working her bottom lip.

"Yeah, but this is you embracing that part of his life that in a very real sense stole him away from you. He chose his dream, his music career over you once." She paused, letting that settle in. "What's to say he won't do it again?" Dani asked.

"Because even then he couldn't escape me. He told me I was always in his thoughts. That he always missed me, every single day. It wasn't as easy for him as I thought it was. And I know he loves me, it's real, and its deep, and I'm really tired of being scared of it," Leigha argued, jumping to Ridge's defense.

"About damn time!" Dani said grinning. "Of course he isn't going to make that mistake again."

"Did you seriously just make me argue my own self-doubt?" Leigha asked, impressed.

"Mmmhhhmm." Dani nodded her head. "Now that you're done being dumb, let's talk about what you're going to wear!"

Chapter Thirty

Standing up from her cushy seat in first class Leigha smiled. It had been a long week without Ridge. He called her every single night, and was always just a text away. But she missed seeing her man. Feeling the warmth of his skin under her fingertips, the way his deliciously masculine smell invaded her senses whenever she was close to him. Of course he was a busy man, and intellectually she completely got that. He had a very full schedule leading up to the award show, press to do, rehearsals, fittings, meetings with the label. It honestly all sounded like a pain in the ass to her, but it was a part of his world, and he seemed to thrive in it. But at night when the shadows danced across her room she stared at them admitting to herself that she wasn't fully herself without him anymore. Maybe she never really was, she just hadn't noticed. The best parts of her reflected the best in him. They were intertwined, at the core of their souls. Leigha didn't want to be that clingy woman that couldn't live a moment without him by her side. But damn it, she missed him.

Grabbing the stylish, but roomy navy zippered oversize tote bag with the black leather straps that she bought specifically for this trip she disembarked the plane with everyone else. Ridge was supposed to send someone to pick her up, since he wasn't exactly the kind of guy who could just hang around an airport unnoticed. Ridge walking around the airport would cause quite a stir. Imagining something close to the hysteria surrounding The Beatles, Leigha found herself laughing thinking about it. Especially since this was Nashville, the hub of country music, and he was one of the most loved artists. The guy in front of her looked over his shoulder at her, wondering what was so funny. She just shook her head at him, he gave her a slightly confused shrug, but he turned back around and kept walking.

It wasn't very hard to spot her ride. He was an absolute mountain of a man, a full head taller than everyone else in the crowded airport, with shoulders wide enough to make a linebacker jealous. To her thinking there were two types of security. The ones that specialized in blending in, so ordinary that your gaze just slid past them without even noticing, and the ones that everyone noticed and knew they would have no problem breaking faces. This guy definitely fell into the latter category. He had wavy hair that he probably thought was brown, but was really bronze, and a full red beard covering his face. As soon as she made eye contact with him he started walking over to her. If he looked intimidating while standing still, it was nothing compared to the vibe he gave off when in motion. Every single muscle working together in tandem like some kind of dangerous predatory grace. Simply put, this was a man that you never wanted to fuck with.

He stopped about a foot away from her, careful not to crowd into her space. "Ms. Taylor? I'm Griff, Ridge sent me." His voice fit the rest of the image perfectly, deep and full, with careful power behind it. Like his natural volume was a few notches louder, and he had to really work to lower it. Leigha was betting when he yelled it would sound like a war lord sending his men into battle. Thinking that maybe she should lay off the romance novels if she was imagining bodyguards as highland lairds from days gone past, she sent him a smile.

"Hi Griff, call me Leigha. So, what's it really like working for Ridge?"

Griff tossed his head back and laughed, surprising her. "He is a pain in my ass most of the time actually. Big bad-ass thinks he is too tough to need protecting."

Griff's whole face had morphed when he laughed, into someone she could see tossing giggling toddlers up in the air at a backyard barbecue. Everyone's favorite big teddy bear of an uncle. Leigha immediately liked him. "If I remember correctly, he never needed any help fighting his battles," she said as they headed off to claim her luggage.

"Oh, he can throw one hell of a punch, sure, and he is the kind of man who doesn't mind getting into a good fight occasionally. But he is precious merchandise now, with a lot at stake. He needs those hands to play his guitar," Griff joked.

"Not to mention that face that scores of women drool over," Leigha said with a wink up at Griff.

"Oh, I like you. You're a feisty one," Griff said picking up her largest suitcase without any effort.

Leigha's cell phone rang as they walked out of the airport into beautiful Tennessee sunshine. She kept walking as she dug it out of her tote bag not even bothering to glance at the screen as she hit accept and brought it to her ear. "Hey baby! I made it here safe and sound, walking out with Griff right now, he didn't have any trouble at all spotting me."

"Didn't figure he would Sugar. I told him to

find the most beautiful woman there and bring her back to me." Leigha abruptly stopped. Her heart felt like it just burst into flames. There was no pain, but there was light bursting through every fiber of her being.

"Ridge," Leigha said softly.

"I know baby, I've really fucking missed you too." His voice hit that low rumble that made her toes want to curl remembering other, more intimate times she had heard it against her skin. "Just a little longer. Remember, you have to meet the stylist first."

"Yeah, we have been emailing back and forth, and have narrowed it down to three dresses. It shouldn't take too long. One will clearly look the best I'm sure." Leigha started moving again, Griff at her side, his gaze traveling around assessing their surroundings. He really was good at his job.

"What about shoes, a bag? Jewelry?" Ridge chuckled when he heard her sigh. "As soon as you get this shit out of the way, then you're all mine for the rest of the night."

"I like the way you think Ridge," Leigha said as Griff opened the door to a big black SUV. Climbing in she told him goodbye and stashed the phone back in her bag.

Griff walked around to the driver's side and got in. "So you are my chauffeur today too?"

He glanced over at her, just a quick flick of his eyes. "I'm a man of many talents."

"I wondered if there would be a driver too," Leigha said honestly. "I'm a little out of my depth with this part of his life." She glanced at the sights as they left the airport. The city was bustling, so full of life.

"If Ridge were here too, there would be another guy to drive," Griff said, this time not taking his eyes off the road.

"So you could focus on guarding his body. But since nobody knows who I am that's not needed," Leigha said nodding her head, getting it.

"Yet," Griff said.

"What?" Leigha asked confused, turning to look at him full on.

"Nobody knows who you are yet. But by tomorrow evening everyone will."

"I doubt anyone will be paying any attention to me," Leigha said. She wasn't trying to put herself down, but this wasn't her world. She was just going to be dipping her toes in the water, not diving in.

"You're a beautiful woman, on the arm of one of the most successful, and recognizable men in this town. Everyone in Nashville will stand up and pay attention, don't doubt that," Griff said.

"Well, shit. No pressure huh," Leigha sighed, her nerves jumping.

"Piece of advice, don't worry about fitting in or trying to be cool, just be authentically yourself. They can think anything they want about you, but don't ever show them you aren't one hundred percent in Ridge's corner. Tearing you apart is only easy to do if you hand them the ammunition. Otherwise, what can they really say? *Oooo, look at that gorgeous woman with him, they clearly love each other.* They're gonna talk anyway and if that's all they got then you smashed it," Griff said wisely.

"Not just a pretty face, are ya Griff." Leigha beamed at him, feeling better. "Thanks." He nodded back, and they rode the rest of the way in a comfortable silence.

Ridge's stylist met them just inside the doors of the mall with a hug. "Leigha, it's so nice to finally meet you!"

"Josie, it is!" Leigha said hugging back. Josie was a tall slim woman, her body full of graceful lines instead of overt curves. She exuded class in a pair of cropped black slacks, bright red ballet flats, and a crisp white blouse. Everything looked pulled together, but effortlessly chic at the same time. Her light brown hair was pulled back in a short ponytail, and her eyes were amazing. One was a light clear blue, and the other was a rich chocolate brown. As far as Leigha could tell there wasn't any makeup on her face, so the focus was on the exotic combination of her eyes.

"I've already got the options set aside for you. But after seeing you in person, I think we need to add one more that caught my eye this morning," Josie said leading the way to the shop of a notable high-end designer. Leigha tried not to gulp at the thought of the cost of the dresses. Correctly reading Leigha, Josie said, "Don't worry. I've been dressing Ridge for years, I've got all his card information on file. You don't even have to think about the money."

"My small town was showing wasn't it?" Leigha joked.

Josie shook her head. "I totally get it. You aren't that kind of woman. I figured that, and honestly if you walked in here and started grabbing one of everything my opinion of you would start slipping drastically. Don't get me wrong, Ridge can definitely afford it, but he really doesn't care about any of this. It's just the trappings for him, his work uniform if you will," Josie said as she weaved through the classy displays towards the discrete dressing rooms in the back.

"I'm not with the celebrity, I'm with the man," Leigha said, the conviction ringing clearly in her voice.

"As someone who cares about him, strictly in the friendly way, I'm glad," Josie said with a smile. She was like a quiet tornado. Sweeping through everything, but leaving no damage in her wake. "Tomorrow night is going to be full of glitz and glam. There will be quite a few women completely bejeweled and bedazzled to the nines. Sequins, rhinestones, the works. That's fine for them, but I think if we put you in something so loud you will lose the essence of who you are. We really don't want that."

"I'm good with simple." Leigha smiled. "And, I'd like Ridge to be able to recognize me."

"Honey, I'd rather have him feel the world tilt on its axis when he lays eyes on you." Josie winked.

"Yes. That. Please." Leigha grinned.

The three dresses they talked about previously were all hung up on the rack inside the dressing area. Leigha tried on the amber colored one first. It was strapless, and hung in a simple column down her body. The color was great for her dark hair and eyes, but made her skin look a little sickly.

"Nope. Maybe if you just got back from vacationing in the tropics, but not today," Josie said shaking her head.

The second one was a poppy red color with a lace overlay across her breasts up to the high neckline. The skirt swept all the way to the floor, but when she turned around her whole back was bare.

"Definitely sexy," Leigha said, turning this way and that looking at different angles in the mirror.

"It is, and you are really pulling it off," Josie said.

"But," Leigha sighed.

"Yep. Exactly, it's not quite right," Josie agreed.

The third one was a clingy black one-shouldered number. There was eye catching beading along the opposite side of the single strap, starting just under her arm and flowing all the way down to the hem.

"I feel a little lopsided," Leigha said with disappointment.

"It looks great on you, but it isn't really you. I can see that." Just then the saleswoman walked in carrying a dress that made Leigha's breath catch in her throat. Josie noticed Leigha's reaction, and smiled. "I had a hunch."

Leigha tried not to rush taking the black dress off, since it probably cost as much as her first car had. But she needed to see that other one, with a desperation that she couldn't explain, but didn't bother questioning.

As soon as she felt the satin brushing against her skin Leigha got chills. She stood there in front of the mirror with her eyes closed just absorbing the way it made her feel. When she finally opened them after a few heartbeats, she just shook her head slowly back and forth. Unable to process what her eyes were telling her. The sapphire blue was completely unadorned. There were no beads, sequins, or anything else to steal attention away from that vibrant color. It hugged the curve of her hips, then flared out at her knees into a mermaid sweep. The deep v neckline hit that perfect balance, showing off just enough of her assets but not too much. There was some kind of fold from the side of her rib cage, climbing the sides of her breasts and behind her head. It framed her breasts, and created this little peekaboo of skin on her side, that thrilled the imagination, but didn't actually show anything.

"Holy shit," Leigha said with a reverent sigh.

"Absolutely. This one will tilt his world. It is classy, and sultry. It barely shows any skin, and yet manages to look sexier than the one showing all the skin," Josie said, her eyes zooming in on each and every detail. Turning to the saleswoman she said. "That dark jeweled clutch. And those charcoal strappy shoes, size..." She looked at Leigha. "Eight."

Leigha nodded her head and continued to stare at her own reflection, enraptured by the dress. The saleswoman hurried away, eager to make the sale.

"Now I think this needs minimal adornment. I'll make the call," Josie said, pulling her cell phone out of the tiny bag she was carrying and stepping away.

Leigha had taken the dress off, and was back in her own clothes when Josie walked back in. "Call to who?" she asked now that she could actually think.

"Ridge asked me to give him a call when you had a dress picked out, and tell him which direction to go in," Josie explained as she gathered up the dress to walk out.

"He isn't," Leigha said, realizing what that meant.

"He totally is. Oh, honey. When your man

wants to buy you jewelry, don't discourage him," Josie laughed.

"I don't need all this though," Leigha said stubbornly.

"Of course you don't, and he knows that, which is probably why he wants to do it for you. Trust me, he did not seem like a man put out just now on the phone," Josie replied.

"True, still. I'm used to providing for myself, handling my own business," Leigha explained.

"I get it. You're a grown ass woman, who can handle her own." Josie nodded. "That's why it's so fun for Ridge to spoil you."

Chapter Thirty-One

The sun was hanging low in the sky when Griff pulled out of the parking lot. It was almost like there was some sort of mystical time suck, no matter how fast you thought you were, every time you left the mall it was always much later than you thought it would be. Maybe it was the lack of windows, and abundance of artificial lighting keeping everything bright as the midday sun. It throws off all sense of time passing, and people will linger longer than they planned. Casinos have also flawlessly harnessed this secret to their advantage.

Leigha watched out the window as the city turned on its neon in the fading light of dusk. The streets and sidewalks they drove past were crowded with people. She noticed a few of them trying to peer into the windows of the SUV as it passed by them. The back was tinted so dark there was no way they would actually be able to see inside, not to mention nobody was even sitting in the backseat. But they didn't know that. Nobody's gaze even lingered on her sitting in the passenger seat though, they had absolutely no idea who she was. That was all going to change tomorrow according to what Griff had told her. It wasn't that she doubted him, she didn't, it still seemed a little surreal to her though. The idea of random strangers knowing who she was. Everyone in her hometown knew her, whether it be through her parents, from school, or seeing her behind the counter at Caffeinated Sprinkles. That was different though, because she knew who they were too. It was a shared knowledge with history weaved between them. This would be all one sided. Her name and face would be carried away on the swiftly moving current of popular culture, gossip rags, and tabloids. Social media, and today's instant society would guarantee that within a few hours people would know everything there was to know about her. With fans on Twitter, Instagram, and Facebook leading the charge. It was all quite overwhelming to think about, and Leigha knew that if she didn't love Ridge so damn much there was no way she would be willing to throw herself on the mercy of the world like that.

A flash of complete understanding whizzed through her mind. This was what made Ridge so willing to come back home to Michigan. He was surrounded by the comfort and protection of home. People who actually knew him, had memories linking them together. It made the inconvenience of being so far away from the epicenter of country music worth it for him. Being able to stop in and grab a coffee or walk down the street without his picture splashed everywhere must have felt like uninhibited freedom to him. He could be himself in the truest sense of the word. Sure, he had fans at home. But nobody was flocking there just to get a glance of his face. People weren't selling maps to his house on the street corners. She always thought he was giving up so much being back in a small town. But now she understood that he was gaining was what really mattered to him.

"Griff, how long have you been looking out for Ridge?" Leigha asked.

"Little over five years now, why?" She could hear the puzzlement coloring his words.

"Just thinking about things. I guess I didn't realize a lot about him being famous. There were people trying to see who was in the car, and I noticed some with cameras perched at the ready. He can't just walk down the street here, not without it making the news," Leigha said with a sigh. "I really never thought of it like that."

"No, he can't. That's why his house is way outside of town, it's the only way he gets any peace here. There are a lot of perks to what he does, and he doesn't take that for granted, but there is a lot that isn't quite so great," Griff said, and there was a darkness to the words letting Leigha know that he didn't like that anymore than she did.

"If he mostly lives in Michigan now where does that leave you? I see him walking around town all the time, and the most that happens is a few people saying hi. He doesn't need protection." Leigha noticed there were fewer and fewer houses passing by outside the windows.

"Even when he isn't here people try to sneak onto the grounds or even into the house. It's best if it isn't left vacant," he admitted.

"So you live there when he is gone?" Leigha asked.

"No, I live there all the time." Griff glanced over at Leigha, and her face must have screamed her thoughts loud and clear. "Don't worry, it's not like I'm in the next room. I live above the garage," he said with a chuckle. "You will have privacy for your reunion."

"It's not, I wasn't, oh hell." Leigha stumbled over her words. Giving up on excuses she finally said, "Thanks." Then thinking about it added, "An apartment above the garage?"

"That makes it sound like I have no space. Ridge likes his toys, and his garage is huge. I have three bedrooms, an office, two bathrooms, kitchen, and a huge living room. I've had my parents and sister over to visit quite a few times. Ridge takes good care of the people he entrusts into his inner circle," Griff told her.

There were no houses visible from the road now, and some of them even had gates. These houses were far enough apart that you might not ever know who you lived next to, which was probably the point. Finally, Griff maneuvered into one of the driveways. He had to stop almost as soon as they made the turn though. There was a tough looking black iron gate blocking their passage. Griff rolled the window down, and Leigha looked over and saw the keypad. She expected him to punch in a code, but he just put his finger on it and the gate swung open.

"Fingerprint reader?" she asked with not a small amount of awe.

"Yeah, tomorrow morning you can come up to my office, and I will get yours added to the system."

"Why have a keypad then?" Leigha asked, full of nerves.

"There are codes to open it too. Also an intercom. Layers of security helps keep people out."

Leigha just nodded her head. The driveway was just as long as the one Ridge had in Michigan. When the trees finally stopped crowding against the drive her breath caught in her throat. This wasn't a house. This was a full-on mansion. It was absolutely huge, and rugged, like a cabin way up in the mountains. There was a lot of wood. Massive timber beams supported the second story porch. There was a large *R* and *B* carved into the beautiful front door. Off to the right was the two-story garage, if it could even be called that. It was almost as big as the house itself was. For as large as it was, and as undoubtedly expensive, there was an ease and comfort about the place. Leigha immediately loved it.

"Holy shit," she whispered.

"Yeah, its sure something," Griff said putting the SUV in park and getting out.

He headed around back and was already unloading her luggage when she managed to climb out. That big, beautiful door swung open, and Ridge stepped out. Boomer came barreling down the front steps toward her, filling the air with the sounds of his joyful barking. Ridge just stood there for a moment, and Leigha remembered pulling up to his other house for the first time. He had been playing guitar sitting on the porch, and she was unsure of her welcome. This time he was standing there with a grin stretched across his face, his eyes shining, and he was just taking her in. Leigha knew without a doubt that he wanted her here this time.

"Sugar," he said, and immediately everything inside of her clenched. Then he was moving, his long legs eating the distance between them in huge chunks.

Leigha launched herself up into his arms as soon as he was close enough, wrapping her arms and legs around him. His mouth landed on hers, and the whole world just flew away. All that held her anchored to this earth was his body pressed up against hers, his mouth moving with hers. Ridge pulled back, resting his forehead against hers. "I don't ever want to be away from you again," Leigha whispered. The words were out of her mouth before she even realized she had thought them.

"That works for me," Ridge said sounding just as breathless as she did. He turned to Griff without bothering to put Leigha down. "Thanks for taking care of my woman, Griff."

"No problem, man," Griff said walking past them, carrying Leigha's luggage into the house. He must have known if left up to them it would stay forgotten in the driveway all night. "See you two tomorrow," Griff said with a knowing chuckle as he walked back out of the house. He got into the SUV heading over towards the garage.

"Bring me inside your house Ridge," Leigha said, her voice dripping with need.

"Yes ma'am, my pleasure," he said as he walked up the steps. Boomer darted inside just before he kicked the door shut. Smart dog.

Leigha didn't even bother trying to look at the house as Ridge carried her through it. All her focus was on the man she loved. It felt like years since she had been in his arms, not just days. The need for him burned with a desperately sharp edge inside of her. She bumped deliciously against his body with every step as he jogged up the stairs. "Hurry," she hungrily said as she kissed every inch of skin she could reach.

"We've got all night baby, I'm not going anywhere," Ridge said.

Leigha moaned, the rumble of his chest had her nipples tightening to peaks inside of her lace bra. "Don't care. Need you now," she said biting into his bottom lip. "Right fucking now."

"Jesus, baby," Ridge groaned, and then she was falling backward with him on top of her.

Leigha felt the soft give behind her, and knew she was in his bed, exactly where she needed to be.

She yanked his shirt up and over his head. Her hands immediately going to the wealth of hot skin she uncovered. Her nails scraped down his chest and over the dips of his abs as she dragged them down towards the waist of his jeans. Ridge's whole body trembled on top of her, and it was everything she needed to know that he was just as crazed with need as she was. She popped the button, pulled the zipper down, and dove inside of his boxer briefs. Her hand wrapped around his dick, and it was like warm steel in her fingers. She pumped him quickly while the other hand pushed his pants down. Finally getting with the *get naked quickly program* Ridge tore her clothes off in a heated frenzy.

Leigha felt almost painfully empty and hollow inside. Her need for him was stronger than her need to draw her next breath. She wrapped her legs around his hips, as he thrust inside of her in one smooth stroke. They both let out groans, the rightness, the feeling of absolute homecoming raging through them. She dug her heels into the muscles of his ass and worked her hips frantically up against his. Her muscles were already quaking deep within her pussy, and she knew he felt it.

"Fuck, I'm not gonna last very long like this Sugar," Ridge said through clenched teeth.

"I don't give a damn. Just fuck me Ridge. I need to feel how much you need me," Leigha said, her hips never stopping their movements.

He let out a growl, an actual growl, and wrapped one hand behind her head, the other snaked underneath her body. He held her pressed to his body and pumped into her harder than he ever had before, Leigha gasped greedily. His face only inches from hers, she could see every last thread holding his control together snap. Her orgasm built bigger and bigger with every demanding slap of his body against hers. Leigha's world had narrowed down to the swirling need in Ridge's eyes, and the feel of him moving inside of her. Her neck wanted to arch back, to ride the freight train of feelings speeding through her, but his hand held her still, making her toes curl instead. Her body exploded with such force that the edges of her vision faded to black. Ridge swallowed the scream that tore out of her mouth with a kiss. His hips went erratic as she pulsed around him, and her nails dug into his shoulders. His whole body shuddered as he moaned into her mouth. Leigha felt the burning heat of his release fill her up, as he finally stilled above her.

They lay there breathless, on top of his bed, floating in the aftermath of the passion. It took a full five minutes before Ridge could manage to roll over and pull out of her. She felt the loss of his body inside hers with a whimper, before curling into his side. Looking up into his eyes she smiled, the way only a woman well pleasured could. He laughed, full and deep. "Welcome to Nashville Sugar."

Chapter Thirty-Two

Ridge's house was a flurry of activity the next day. Josie was at the door with a whole entourage bright and early with the singular goal of polishing the both of them until they shone like the star that Ridge actually was. Sitting on a stool in the guest bedroom, Leigha decided that she was just going to enjoy it, and go along even though it wasn't really her thing. The flamboyant makeup artist, Jonathan, asked her what her daily beauty routine consisted of, as he started unpacking his massive case, which to her mind held more makeup than the Sephora that Dani liked to drag her into whenever they made it to the mall back home.

"Umm, not much actually. Moisturizer, some minty lip balm. If I'm getting fancy I'll add a swipe or two of mascara. But I'm usually out the door pretty early in the mornings, to open my coffee shop, and I'd rather sleep the extra few minutes," Leigha admitted with a shrug.

He stood staring at her a moment, clearly trying to collect his thoughts. "Well, you have great skin, so you don't really need much. We're gonna be putting a hell of a lot more on you today though, hun. All of the cameras practically require it. But we will keep you looking as fresh as possible," Jonathan said with a smile.

"No smoky eye?" Leigha grinned at him, joking around.

"Not this time, but girl, you could so totally pull it off," he replied with a sassy wink. "I will keep it in mind for the next event you need me to glam you up for."

Leigha zoned out while Jonathan painted her nails a delicate, understated shade of pink. The hairstylist, Christine was busy conferring with Josie about what to do with her hair.

"Well, the dress already makes quite a statement. Jonathan is going for fresh and natural, we don't want to over complicate her hair and ruin the whole look," Josie said.

"What about a fishtail braid off to the side? Some careless pieces escaping around her face?" Christine asked while lifting her hair off to the side to demonstrate.

"I like that, Leigha, what do you think?" Josie asked after a minute of intense consideration.

"I braid my hair quite often, although a fishtail, I've never mastered that one. I think that will help me to still look like myself, just a little more glam than usual," Leigha said, then smiled. "And Ridge has a thing about my braid."

"Of course he does, men just can't wait to unbind it, and get their hands through all those strands," Jonathan said as he painted her toenails.

All three women stared at him, a little awestruck. "What? I might be gay, but the appeal isn't lost on me," he said with a careless shrug of his shoulders.

"Guess that settles it then." Josie laughed. "I'll be back, I've got to go check in with Ridge."

"I'd think he is a pro at this thing by now," Leigha said.

"Oh he is, but he still gets nervous, especially when he is performing a new song for the first time at one of these things. That gets to him more than being up for an award," Josie said as she walked out of the room.

Leigha sat there thinking about that. It helped her a little that she wasn't the only one nervous about tonight. All she had to do was walk next to Ridge and sit down to enjoy the show. He was the one who had to get up there and do something. Just thinking of finally being the one on his arm while he lived his dream settled most of the nerves. It was actually kind of nice not having to worry about the details. Letting the glam squad, as she thought of them, do their thing she relaxed.

They had her looking like a goddess in far shorter time than she would have thought possible. She was still staring at herself in the mirror when Ridge walked up behind her. She watched him look his fill at her reflection. She could see exactly how much he liked her dress, his pupils dilating.

"You're the most gorgeous woman in the whole damn world, and nobody will be able to take their eyes off of you tonight. I'm so lucky that I get to be the one who has you on my arm. Reminds me of how I felt waiting in the foyer at your parents' house. Watching you walk down the stairs in your prom dress. I swear my heart leapt right out of my body and fell at your feet," Ridge said softly.

"You stared at me for the longest time. I started to wonder if I had a booger hanging out of my nose!" Leigha laughed. "I'd never seen you look at me quite like that before."

"No, you just left me speechless Sugar, every single thought in my head just emptied out. You're the only one who's ever done that to me."

"Ever?" Leigha asked, needing to hear it again.

"Ever ever," Ridge whispered in her ear. Wrapping his arms around her, he turned her to face him. "It's not a corsage this time, but I've got something to complete your dress."

Leigha thought of the flowers he slid on her wrist all those years ago, and smiled at him. "No corsage? Well, I suppose I can manage without one."

Ridge pulled a velvet box out of his pocket, and watching her face he slowly raised the lid. Nestled inside was a pair of sapphire earrings, tear drops that reminded her of the way Lake Michigan looked in the winter. Deep, and sparkling blue. Tears gathered in her eyes, and she blinked, trying to keep them from falling and ruining the makeup Jonathan worked so hard on. Ridge pulled the matching bracelet from the box and put it on her right wrist. Looking down at it she turned her hand and watched as the stones caught the light.

"Ridge, these are too much," Leigha whispered in a trembling voice.

"No, Sugar, they're not. I know you don't give a damn about my money, hell you loved me when all I could afford for a date was a picnic in the back of my truck."

"Best memories of my life, don't ever doubt that," Leigha interrupted.

"I don't," he said cupping the side of her face. "Which is why it's nice to be able to give you more now. Because you wouldn't have cared if I never could have. I would still have been enough for you." Mindful of her lipstick, he leaned in and pressed a gentle kiss on her. "Put the earrings on, I want to see them," he said handing them to her.

Leigha smiled and slid the hooks through the holes in her ears and posed for him. "What do you think? Am I ready for this?"

"They won't know what hit them." He offered her his arm like a gentleman. "Come on, I can't wait to show you off, then when we get back home I'm gonna fuck you in nothing but those sapphires tonight," he said into her ear, and Leigha trembled all over in anticipation.

Chapter Thirty-Three

"Deep breath Sugar," Ridge said as the limousine pulled to a stop. The world lurking outside the dark tint of the window was an absolute frenzy. Leigha nodded her head resolutely, Ridge gave the window a quick tap, and the door was pulled open. Griff, dressed in a nice suit grinned at them and Ridge stepped out into the chaos of lights. As the flashes went off, he held his hand out and Leigha grasped it in hers as she did her best to step gracefully out. There was a heart stopping gasp that sounded collectively through the whole crowd. The sight of her leaving everyone stunned momentarily, before they recovered enough to start lobbing questions at the two of them with increasing persistence.

"Who's the lady with you, Ridge?"

"Looks like you've moved on already, Ridge."

"Does Suzy know you brought a date tonight, Ridge?"

"Give her a kiss for the camera's Ridge?"

"Who are you wearing?"

"When's your next single coming out?"

"How do you feel about having caught the most eligible bachelor in country music?"

Ridge wrapped his arm around Leigha in solidarity and gave her the tiniest of squeezes. Leigha knew nobody would have been able to see it, he just wanted to comfort her in the face of the media onslaught. He might be used to this, but she certainly had no experience with it. They were steered swiftly past the paparazzi flashes towards television cameras, and eager hosts waiting impatiently with predatory smiles and microphones held at the ready. The red carpet felt an awful lot like what navigating a rocky pass in a sailboat must have. You knew there were sharks lurking everywhere just waiting to gleefully tear into you should you make one wrong move. There was no way to go around, you just had to find the courage to power through, with a smile as your armor, and balls of steel. Well, Leigha was no wimp. She could handle this. Setting her shoulders, she stood up straight, put her best 'bless your heart' smile on, the one she used with annoying customers at Caffeinated Sprinkles, and sent Ridge a wink. The smile he flashed her was sure to melt the panties off every woman in at least a three-square mile radius, but she knew he got her message. The first perky host all but attacked them as they approached.

"Ridge Bradley, aren't you looking spectacular tonight! You're up for only one award, you're scheduled to perform, and rumor has it that it will be a brand new song we haven't heard before. Can you tell us anything about the song?"

"Thanks. I'm glad to be here, I've always had a really good time at this show every year, I've been very blessed to be so embraced in this business, by the fans, and the industry. As for what song I'm gonna sing tonight, I guess you just have to wait and see like everyone else," Ridge said in a teasing voice.

Not missing a beat the woman honed in on Leigha with a patronizing glare. Leigha got the impression the previous questions were only to soften Ridge up, because the gleam in her eyes clearly communicated how much she wanted this. "Who's this lovely lady on your arm Ridge? A date for tonight, or are you debuting a budding romance to the world?" She pointed the microphone in Ridge's face, and Leigha held her breath.

"This beauty, that I don't deserve, but am lucky enough to bring along tonight is Leigha Taylor," Ridge said, and Leigha could hear how proud he was to say that.

"Are you an up-and-coming singer we should

be on the lookout for Leigha?" the woman asked, directing the microphone towards her.

Ridge leaned in before Leigha had a chance to think of a response. "Nope, Leigha isn't in show business at all."

"How did you catch this hunk's attention then Leigha? I'd imagine it's pretty difficult to get close to someone like him." The words 'gold digger' were left unspoken, but Leigha clearly heard them all the same.

"Well, she was the prettiest girl I'd ever seen. It took a while to finally get her to agree to go on a date with me, but I knew I was the luckiest sixteen-year-old on the planet when she finally did," Ridge said leaning in and kissing Leigha on the temple through his smile.

"Wait, sixteen? Ridge Bradley are you seriously telling us that you ran back into the arms of your high school sweetheart after divorcing Suzy Cordell? Had the two of you kept in touch the whole time? Is that where things between you two went wrong?" This time the host didn't have to feign shock. The surprise on her face was as real as it got, probably the only genuine thing about the lady.

"No, we certainly didn't. When Ridge set out for Nashville to follow his dreams, I went to college and followed mine. That was the last I heard from him until I bumped into him after he bought a house back in our hometown quite recently," Leigha said defending Ridge. She didn't like the assumption that Ridge had her waiting in the wings through his marriage. He may have been unable to extricate her from his heart, but she certainly wasn't in his life.

"And the sparks flew again, how adorable," the host said, her voice all but dripping in artificial sweetness. Leigha half expected her shoes to be sticking to the floor she was laying it on so thick.

"What can I say, that pretty girl grew up to be one hell of a beautiful woman," Ridge said before easing them away to the next host absolutely starving for the exclusive. They all but repeated the same conversation over and over as they made their way achingly slowly inside. Leigha was exhausted, and the awards ceremony hadn't even technically started yet.

"Is it always like that?" she whispered.

"Like a mad house?" Ridge asked. "Yeah."

"Why does everyone seem to think everything about your life is their business? Don't they realize how rude that is?" Leigha asked, annoyed.

"They just don't care. The assumption is the moment I signed the dotted line on my recording contract all of me belongs to the spotlight," Ridge said, and there was a distinct jaded edge to his voice.

"It's a high price to pay for a dream," Leigha said weaving her fingers through his.

"Being rich and famous is expensive to the soul," he said as they made their way to their seats.

Leigha expected them to be a few rows back since like the shark lady had pointed out he was only nominated for one award tonight, and not really expected to win it. But they were front and center. Leigha sat down with a look at Ridge. He correctly read the confusion on her face.

"They're hoping to catch some drama on camera. Suzy is only a few seats away, and they want us in the same frame."

"You mean expect you two to stand up and start screaming at each other right in the middle of the show?" Leigha glanced around and he was right. Most everyone was staring at the two of them.

"Sure, that would get great ratings for them. But seeing heart breaking reactions from her when she sees you would too. No matter what we do tonight, just by being in the same room it's going to make headlines."

"I know just how much it hurts to see you with another woman. Now I'm the weapon instead of the one being crushed," Leigha sighed.

"I'm sorry Sugar, I wasn't trying to dangle her in front of you anymore than I'm trying to hurt her by bringing you." Leigha could see a muscle in Ridge's jaw tick, letting her know just how much he disliked the idea of causing pain.

"I know. I wouldn't have come if I thought you wanted me here as some revenge on your ex-wife. But I guess no matter what, there is no good time to see your ex with someone else." Ridge just nodded his head. Her heart went out to him, because she knew he wasn't taking any pleasure in parading her in front of his ex-wife. He said that he didn't love Suzy enough when they were married, and this is only going to bring that point home.

Sitting in the audience during an awards show was vastly different than watching it at home, Leigha learned. The cameras moving all over the place, meant that she rarely had a great view. They paused the ceremony for commercial breaks, and it was a flurry of activity. People rushing for the bathrooms, or backstage for the next segment. As soon as someone got up from their seat a filler would be there to sit down, so none of the seats appeared empty. It was like well-orchestrated chaos. At the third commercial break Ridge got up to head backstage and get ready for his performance. Leaning in he kissed her forehead, then whispered in her ear, "I can't wait for you to hear this song, Sugar."

As he walked off, some guy sat down in his place. "Hi, when the cameras turn back on, we're supposed to look like friends, okay?"

Leigha just nodded her head, not really caring if she looked friendly with the stranger for the cameras. She was here for Ridge, and after what he whispered to her she couldn't wait to hear what he was about to sing. The commercial break ended, and they launched into the award for group performance of the year. The whole time the nominees were listed the nervous energy was bubbling up inside of Leigha. When the lucky winners were up thanking their fans, God, and each other it was all she could do to sit still in her seat. Twice she caught her foot tapping, and had to stop herself.

Another mega popular country superstar walked forward to thunderous applause. Giving his trademarked charming smile he said, "This next artist doesn't really need an introduction, but, that's why they've got me up here tonight in front of y'all." He paused a moment for the chuckle that ran through the audience. "So here to sing his brand-new song, that he told me backstage was the most honest one he has ever written, is Ridge Bradley with *Still Yours!*"

All the air left Leigha's body in a rush. Her hands were shaking like leaves in the wind. The lights went down, and the curtain rose, and Ridge stood there alone. There was no backup band. It was just him in a pair of scuffed boots, well-worn jeans, and a plain black t shirt, holding his acoustic guitar. He looked right at Leigha, his eyes burning with intensity, took a step up to the microphone, and started playing. She knew without a single doubt that he was wearing that casual outfit up there, for a reason. It wasn't to appeal as the approachable every-man, like his image portrayed. Every single person in the audience, in the whole damn world, knew that he was singing the song just for Leigha.

I wish you knew how many nights I've lain awake
Your name playing in my head
Just like a song stuck on repeat
Over and over
Over and over
Years have passed, oh love
Not a day I'll forget
But I'm still yours
Yours to have

Yours to hold
Yours to love in the dark
Just yours
This heart will forever be
Still Yours
I've been yours since I was sixteen, Sugar
When we had everything all figured out
My arms were made for holding you tight
You're all that is ever been right
When I'm an old man heading to my grave
I'll know I've spent my life right if I can say
That I'm still yours

Leigha had tears running unchecked down her face. She didn't give a damn if her heart was on full display for the cameras. All that mattered to her was the man standing up on that stage laying his whole heart at her feet for everyone in the entire world to see. He finished the song and there was a moment of pure silence, not a single person even dared breathe, before the whole audience rose as one and cheered for him. But Leigha knew all Ridge could see was her. He pressed his hand over his heart, still staring into her eyes before giving a little bow and walking back off the stage. She sat back down with everyone else, but she wasn't in the moment anymore. Her head was full of Ridge. He put words he had spoken to her in a song. He even wore the same clothes as the night he showed up on her doorstep and tore her life wide open again.

Chapter Thirty-Four

The rest of the awards ceremony flew past in a dreamy haze for Leigha. As predicted, he didn't win the award he was up for, it went to the guy who had introduced him before his performance. Ridge seemed pretty happy for him though, so Leigha knew they must actually be friends. She couldn't muster up enough excitement for the goings on though, when her man had poured his heart out to her in front of the whole world. Ridge was a man accustomed to being on display, but he had taken it to a whole new level tonight. She wasn't able to show him just how much that song had meant to her like she really wanted to. A lingering kiss when he returned to his seat, and some whispers in his ear wasn't nearly enough. Finally it was over, and everyone started to leave. Most of them were going to one after party or another, to be photographed hanging out with the night's big winners, and talk about the times they had won awards themselves. Leigha thought they were heading to one of them too, but Ridge told her he only wanted to spend the rest of his night with her, just her. It had chills racing through her body when he said it a moment ago, and as Leigha walked into the ladies' room, she still felt them.

With so many people in the building Leigha expected there to be a line to use the toilet, as was so often the case with ladies' public restrooms. But this was a small one, only three stalls off to one side, and the other held a posh mirrored seating area with a pair of love seats. It seemed like it had dual purposes, you could touch up your makeup, and gather your nerves before facing the crowd.

Leigha was finishing up drying her hands at the sink when the door finally opened, and someone else joined her in the room. She looked up in the mirror to see who it was, as you do in those situations. Just a quick glance, barely a second, but it was enough. All the air whooshed out of her lungs. Suzy Cordell, Ridge's ex-wife stood there in all her stunning glamorous glory, staring back at her looking just as surprised to see Leigha, as she was to see Suzy. Leigha was the first one to recover. She settled her face into careful blankness. It was polite, but hopefully gave absolutely nothing that she was thinking inside, away on the outside.

Suzy shook her head back and forth slowly. Leigha had a moment to think this wasn't going to go well. "It's nice to finally, actually, really meet you Leigha. I feel like I've known you for so damn long," Suzy said with a brilliant, and completely genuine smile.

The confusion on Leigha's face was clear. Gone was the carefully arranged poker face she had been striving for only moments ago. "What? I'm sorry, I just don't understand."

With a shrug Suzy said, "Ridge never seemed to sleep very well. At first I thought it was just the adrenaline from performing, then I thought it was when his mind was the most creative. It didn't take me very long to figure out that it wasn't either of those. I used to wake up in the middle of the night and find him sitting alone in the dark, sometimes it was the living room, but more often than not it was outside on the back porch. He had that old beat-up guitar on his lap, and he would be lazily strumming on it looking up at the stars. I thought it was a melody he was working out, a little something that was rolling around in his head. That happens to me sometimes when I'm trying to write songs," she added as an afterthought, as she sat down on one of the love seats. "But it was always the same. It never turned into one of the songs he wrote. Eventually I started calling it Leigha's song, not out loud of course, just in my head. Sometimes I would just linger and listen, since he didn't know I was there. He would just play that little melody over and over, and the look on his face was so damn raw that it broke my heart. I always knew that you were still there, down deep in his heart, from the first time he talked about growing up in Michigan. He used to stumble over your name, like just saying it caused him real physical pain. But I didn't understand, not really, until after we were married and I watched him mourn your loss in a million tiny ways every day, that he wasn't ever gonna be over you. Some people just never get over their first love, and that's what lots of people want. How many songs, books, and movies are written about it, countless right?"

Leigha sat down across from Suzy, drawn in by the woman's vulnerable honesty. This was not the catty confrontation she had been hoping to avoid at all costs. "I honestly didn't know. I thought he looked so happy with you, in all the pictures. It killed me to see the two of you splashed all over magazines and the news. I couldn't walk through the store without seeing everything I had lost staring back at me every time I tried to buy groceries. I never reached out, or contacted him in any way. Never. Please know that. No matter how much it hurt me, I wouldn't do that to someone's marriage."

"I know. I wouldn't be here right now telling you this if you had. But just because you weren't actually there, doesn't mean you weren't there. Ya know? That little melody he used to play to the moon? I got to hear the full song tonight, and it was beautiful, honestly, it left me speechless," Suzy added at Leigha's doubtful expression. "I always loved Ridge, even when he didn't love me enough. And I wanted his happiness, even if it wasn't with me. That's not to say it doesn't hurt too, it does. I'm going to shed a few tears, probably more than a few. But I understand now, better than I did when he told me that he couldn't stay married to me anymore, that this is what is right. He was meant to be with you. I never really had him, not the best part of him. That has been yours since he was a teenager. I was just borrowing him for a little while, I guess." There were tears shimmering in Suzy's blue eyes now, and she blinked rapidly a few times to keep them from slipping down her face. "Do me a favor? Don't take him for granted, okay? Because being loved like that, the way he loves you is so damn rare. Ridge isn't a perfect man, but he is one of the few good ones, and if you break his heart he will never, ever be whole again. You are the sun his whole universe revolves around. I'm gonna have that someday too, damn it," she said with a fierceness that made Leigha hope it was true. Suzy stood up, so Leigha did too. "Have a good night Leigha, and congratulations," she said hugging her.

"Thank you, I really mean it. Thank you, Suzy," Leigha said, still absorbing everything that she had just heard. It wasn't until Suzy drifted back out the door, her face perfectly composed and showing none of the raw honesty from only moments ago, that Leigha wondered what it was that she was congratulating her for.

Chapter Thirty-Five

Leigha wished they could have managed to sneak out without running into any of the photographers waiting to pounce. But they were packed around every single door, even staff entrances, should any of the celebrities in attendance dare to think about trying to make a covert escape. But Ridge led her out with a confident smile on his face, and a protective arm around her, making it as quick and painless as possible. He clearly had loads of practice with throngs of photographers dogging his steps. Leigha was grateful that he didn't stop for interviews, and he didn't pose for pictures though. They would have to take whatever shots they got of the couple walking out the door or climbing into the backseat and make do. The press might have been disappointed in that, but Leigha definitely wasn't.

They didn't say much to each other during the ride home, but the silence wasn't tense or loaded. It had settled comfortably around them, making the rest of the world fade away, and Leigha savored the moment tucked up next to the man she loved. She knew she should tell Ridge about seeing Suzy, and she would, but she didn't want to right now. This was their time, it felt special, and she wasn't about to spoil that. The car slowed to a smooth stop in front of Ridge's house, and he got out, automatically holding his hand out to help her exit. It was awkward to get out of the backseat in the dress she was wearing, and Leigha was grateful for the assistance. Leigha couldn't help but think of Ridge holding his hand out to help her out of his pickup truck at their senior prom, and the memory warmed her soul and had a smile stretching across her face. So much had changed since then, but some things never would. It felt good to look back at all those moments and smile, instead of having to shut them down and quickly push them away to avoid the rush of pain that used to come with them.

Ridge led her up the step and held his front door open for her to walk in ahead of him. After all the highs of the night Leigha expected him to turn around and shove her back against the door and rip her dress off in the rush to get to her skin. But he surprised her when he said, "I'm gonna sit out on the back porch for a while. Why don't you go on and get out of that dress, as lovely as it looks on you, I'm sure it isn't the most comfortable. Meet me out there in a few?" He ran a finger softly under her jaw as he said it, sending shivers racing through her body. Leigha nodded her head in a daze, and turned to head towards his bedroom, but Ridge caught her hand in his and turned her back around before she could even make it a full step. "Leave the jewelry on though Sugar," he said with a smirk and a quick teasing kiss on her neck.

This time Leigha was grinning as she walked away. That man. He sure could send her hormones into an uproar with his smirk, and his kiss, hell if she even started to think about everything else he could do to her she wouldn't make it into the bedroom. And he definitely knew it. Ridge was not a man clueless to his effect on his woman. Leigha saw the hanger waiting on the front of the closet door and shimmied out of the dress with a sigh. Hanging it up she said a tiny thanks to Josie for the forethought to leave the hanger out in the open. It would be a shame to ruin the dress by tossing it in the corner. Having it ripped off her would be acceptable but leaving it in a heap on the floor wasn't. Thinking about that had Leigha laughing as she set the hanger back on the closet door. Standing there in her underthings and the jewelry she wondered what Ridge meant by comfortable. She didn't exactly plan on spending the rest of the evening playing scrabble with him. Sweats were out, not that he wouldn't peel them off her, but nobody felt powerful in them. She decided to leave the sexy lace on. The blush pink lace was so delicate that it hid nothing, and just thinking about the way Ridge's eyes would burn when he looked at her in it had wetness pooling between her legs. He sure did love her in pink lace.

Walking into the closet she grabbed the first thing her hand landed on and pulled it off the rack. She brought it to her face for a moment and savored the softly lingering scent of Ridge that never seemed to wash completely out of his clothes. It was an old faded denim shirt that just about swallowed her whole. Not bothering to button more than the center one, just enough to stop it from sliding off her shoulders, Leigha walked out of the bedroom to find her man. In Michigan she would have turned into a popsicle on the porch wearing just that, but here in Nashville it was quite a bit warmer, and she was counting on Ridge to offer his body heat if she got cold.

Standing by the glass she stopped and watched him. He wasn't sitting there relaxing like she thought he would be, he was standing at the edge of the porch, his shoulders stiff and tense. Wondering if he had gotten a phone call with bad news in the last few minutes Leigha opened the door and walked the short distance to Ridge. Wrapping her arms around his middle she laid her head in that perfect spot just in between his shoulder blades. "What's wrong baby?"

Ridge shook his head, "I can play in front of thousands of people, and the nerves don't get to me. I fly high on all that energy. But you, Leigha Taylor, you have the power to absolutely terrify me." He turned around in her arms burying his face in the side of her neck and took a shaky breath.

"I guess that makes us even then. You terrify me all the time too Ridge Bradley," Leigha said staring up at him with a small smile.

Ridge leaned his head back and laughed. "Only you have ever made me feel like this. The biggest mistake I ever made was walking away from you."

"I don't know Ridge, I think now that it happened the way it was supposed to. Life follows its own course, and that's not always the quickest, or easiest, but it's always the right one," Leigha said thinking that if he hadn't walked away they wouldn't have grown into the people they were now. "Besides, we can't change what happened in the past. I'm just happy we're together now."

"You're right, and I'm messing this all up." He took a step backwards, away from her. "I've gone over this a thousand different times in my head. All the things I wanted to say to you, all the ways I could make this special and memorable for you. But none of them seem right. Now that I'm standing here in this moment with you, I don't want to say any of that shit." Ridge dropped down to one knee and stared up at Leigha with everything he felt written in the beautiful green of his eyes. "I've loved you as long as I can remember, and I can promise you that will never stop. I need you to marry me Leigha, because I don't plan on ever giving you up."

Leigha stood there staring down at Ridge, trying to think about the words coming out of his mouth. Tears slid down her cheeks and she nodded her head slowly.

"Yeah? You're gonna be my wife?" Ridge asked, his own eyes glossy with tears.

"Yes," Leigha whispered.

Ridge jumped up grabbing Leigha's face in his hands and kissed her. Leigha wrapped her arms around his shoulders and gave him everything she had inside. He pulled back enough to rest his forehead against hers, "I've got a ring, I was supposed to hold it when I asked you, but I forgot I was so nervous."

"I don't care. It was perfect, because it wasn't perfect. It was real. I'm so glad you didn't plan a huge production. All I need is you Ridge," Leigha said tunneling her fingers up into the back of his hair. "All I've ever needed is you."

Ridge leaned down to take her mouth again, this time he kissed her with a hunger that stole her breath in its intensity. His hands left her face and before Leigha could protest the lack of contact they were gripping her waist. Knowing exactly what he wanted she wrapped her legs around him, trusting that Ridge had her. And he did, he always did. He walked them the few feet over to the seating arrangement in the corner of the porch. Ignoring the two chairs he sat Leigha down on the plush loveseat. Down on his knees he was eye to eye with her and recognizing the look in them Leigha waited to see what he would do next. Her heart was beating fast, and the anticipation was a delicious torture. His eyes on hers he reached up and pushed the button from its hole, then he pulled the sides of the shirt apart, and off her shoulders. His eyes burned a scorching path over her body, taking in the see-through scraps of blush lace barely covering her.

"Damn Sugar, seeing you like this, it never

gets old," Ridge said. His voice deep and rough with passion.

"That's a good thing since you just asked to be the one seeing me exactly like this for a long time," Leigha said lost in his eyes.

"For the rest of my life, and not a moment sooner," Ridge said as he reached into his pocket. He pulled out the box, and she immediately recognized it as the same place he got the bracelet and earrings she still had on. He opened it, and her breath caught at the sight of the ring nestled inside. It wasn't dripping with millions of stones, or over the top the way so many of them are. There was a large princess cut diamond solitaire shining up from its platinum setting. It was everything Leigha had never dared to dream of. She wasn't a flashy woman, and Ridge understood that about her. This ring would never look out of place on her finger, even in her jeans and Caffeinated Sprinkles t-shirts behind the counter serving coffee. Classic and completely timeless, it would also look just as good fifty years from now. Leigha held her left hand out, and it was shaking as Ridge slid the ring onto her finger.

Leigha thought about the fact that she was literally dripping with jewels from him now, and smiled. Ridge was a man who liked seeing his mark on her, and right now his mark was the stones. Sitting up she ran her hands under her breasts slowly. Ridge's eyes watched her transfixed as she unlatched the front hook of her bra. She grazed her own nipples as she slid the cups off her breasts, and goosebumps broke out along her skin at the sound of Ridge's breath quickening. Pulling the bra off she tossed it aside. Her skin felt hot and needy, and she almost laughed remembering thinking about the temperature. There was no need for his body heat with the desire burning through her blood. Leigha cupped her breasts, teasing herself a moment, like she used to do alone in her bedroom late at night. Giving them a squeeze, she let her hands slide forward until she was pinching her nipples. The moan bubbling up out of her throat was just as much from his growl as her own sensations. She let her hands continue roaming across her skin as they headed downwards. "How come you still have all your clothes on Ridge?" she asked him as she played with the top of the lace stretching across her lower stomach.

Her question seemed to surprise him, and it took a second for it to filter through the haze of lust in his brain. Once it did, Ridge wasted no time in shedding his clothes, all of them. It made her smile at the sight of his dick proudly stretching away from his body. He was already thick with need, and as she watched a shiny pearl of pre-cum escaped the tip. "Don't stop now Sugar, you were just getting to the good part," Ridge said kneeling back down in front of her.

With a seductive smile she opened her legs wider, and ran her fingers down between them. Feeling her wetness through the lace she teased herself, tracing her lips back up, but not touching her clit, even though it was practically crying out for it.

"How wet is your pussy right now?" Ridge asked, his voice so low that she didn't really hear it, but she saw his lips move and she knew what he said.

Making another pass along her slit she watched his eyes, this time she gave in to temptation, and stopped to make tiny circles over her clit. "Soaked through the lace," she finally answered him, without stopping the teasing circles.

With a growl Ridge gripped the front of the panties and ripped them right down the center, revealing her pussy. Leigha had moved her hands when the lace ripped away from her, but it felt so good that she immediately put her hand back. "That's right, don't stop now," she heard him say.

But she felt so good that she couldn't stop now if she tried. His eyes kept flicking back and forth between her quick fingers, and her own eyes. She knew hers must look just as sex drunk as his did, and that turned her on even more. Her breath was coming in quick little pants now, as the pressure swirled deep down inside of her.

"I'm so empty Ridge," she moaned, her legs starting to tremble.

"I know Sugar," he said pulling her to the edge of the cushion. As her fingers were busy racing towards that feeling flooding through her Ridge ran his dick across the opening of her pussy. She moaned and arched into him, but he backed up just out of reach.

"Want you inside of me baby," she whimpered.

"Not yet," Ridge said. His teeth were clenched, showing her that he was teasing himself just as much as he was teasing her. Rocking back into her he slid his dick between her lips, just inside the entrance. He gripped her hips in his hands to prevent Leigha from arching up into him again and filling her emptiness. She could feel the heat from his dick, and it felt so deliciously warm that she wanted nothing more than to feel it deep inside of her. Thinking about how good he felt inside, how he filled her completely, and always stretched her to fit his thickness had the first flutters starting. Leigha slowed her fingers down, and made herself wait for the orgasm hovering in her, dragging it out until she saw the frustration in Ridge's eyes. She wanted him right there, just as desperate for her to come as she was. When he groaned, and his fingers dug tighter into her hips she knew he was there. Looking into his eyes, she pinched her clit hard, and broke apart in a rush that bathed the head of his dick.

Ridge surged forward, finally giving her what she wanted. His eyes still holding hers, refusing to let go. She could feel every single glorious inch of him locked inside of her as she pulsed around him. Ridge didn't give her a moment to catch her breath, he thrust into her fast and hard. His body pressed tight up against hers, leaving her hand stuck between them. Every movement of his hips pushed her fingers against her already sensitive clit. It was almost too much for Leigha, and she screamed out into the night as the second orgasm ripped through her. She felt Ridge tense up, and follow her over that narrow edge into bliss.

"I don't want to wait to have you as my wife Leigha," he whispered, his body still twitching inside of hers, his eyes raw with feeling.

"Me either," Leigha said.

"Let's elope. Immediately," Ridge said with her favorite smirk.

A Note From The Author

Thank you so much for choosing Ridge and Leigha's love story...

This couple has meant so much to me this year while I wrote their story, and I'm happy to finally be able to share them with you!

I hide tiny little pieces of my own life in everything I write, and this one is no exception.

I hope you have enjoyed reading it just as much as I loved writing it for you.

If you're interested in reading more, and I really hope you are, please check out my other works.

You can keep up with me on Twitter, and Pinterest at @CaraRomanAuthor, or on Facebook at @AuthorCaraRoman.

Keep an eye out for more titles, and I look forward to seeing you soon!

xoxoxo

~Cara

About The Author

Hi, thanks for reading my book!

Hi, I'm Cara, which is my pen name, but I think of Cara as the most intimate and genuine part of who I am. I live in Michigan with my family, and our fabulously sassy dog. I drink far too much coffee, read all the books I can, hoard makeup, swear more than my mother would like, and dance around my kitchen -poorly- while I cook.

Find me on social media @CaraRomanAuthor! I have zero chill, and LOVE to connect with my readers. It's kind of the best thing ever.

Other Books By Cara Roman

Definitely Memorable

Caitlyn has always dreamed of vacationing in Ireland. After a disappointing divorce she decides its time she does something for herself. What she didn't count on was meeting a charming and devastatingly handsome Irishman, Nolan in a pub. Unable, or unwilling to deny the chemistry between them she throws caution to the wind embarking on a whirlwind romance. Love is never as simple as it seems though, and hers takes a course she never could have predicted.

Without A Wolf
(Big Woods Pack Book One)

New in town, Emma Lowe was hiding a big secret. Wolf shifter Kian Decker needed to find out who she was, and why she was so very appealing to him. Turns out Emma wasn't the only one in town with secrets. Now their lives have been turned upside down, and they need to figure where they stand.

Running From The Wolf
(Big Woods Pack Book Two)

The second book in the Big Woods Pack series, Kayla Decker spent years being mad at Lex Kolter. Using her anger as a shield to keep Lex at bay isn't working so well since the shake ups in the pack. Just when they stop fighting each other new information comes to light threatening the pack once again.

Other Books From Baying Hound Media

Tell-Tale Hearts
by H.A. Blackwood

Darcy Ford is coming off an ill-advised relationship that ended in disaster. When she's at her lowest point, she meets a woman who takes her back ten years to a night of wild passion. A night when she met-and lost-someone who opened new worlds to her. A night where her heart was stolen. A night which was the beginning of this most recent disastrous affair. Only by re-telling these tales can she find her way back to her lost love and the return of her heart.

Candid Camera
by H.A. Blackwood

A new relationship. A secret from the past. Will their love survive?

Darcy Ford and Gemma Amante are contemplating the next big move in their relationship when Ashleigh, a lover from Gemma's past, shows up unexpectedly. She brings news that has Darcy and Gemma on a trip to Los Angeles.

Gemma's friends from her old life as a sex worker are in trouble and need help. Going undercover as sex cam workers in the city of sin may seem like a literal pleasure trip, but when they go up against a new type of criminal, they're going to need all of their sexy savvy. Between steamy escapades, clues begin to emerge. If they're going to solve this mystery, they'll have to risk their way of life, their relationship, and their very lives.

Adored: A Collection Of Poetry
Volume One
by H.A. Blackwood

Whimsical. Fantastical. Celestial.

The poems in this book reflect a lot of different things, but they all have one thing in common: you'll wish they were written about you. You'll wish this was a permanent tribute to you, the reader, on display for the world to see.

Such is the magic of the written word. It can bring out many emotions, but the one you'll be left with after reading this book is simply this: adored.